"If you write anything about me, I'll sue."

Merry's tone was inflexible, but she wasn't sure how Lee would react. He was sitting on the sand, close to where she knelt—too close for comfort.

"You can sue me if you want," Lee said, "but what I write or don't write is not the problem. You're afraid of the way I feel about you. You're afraid of the way you feel about me."

"And *you* are afraid you won't get the information you need.... Well, easy come, easy go, Mr. Zurbaron. And I am going."

She started to rise, but he pulled her into his arms. His mouth claimed hers with a reckless fever. Then, just as Merry thought she would lose control, Lee pulled away.

"Can't you see what we have together?" he urged. "I *know* you feel it, too. Sooner or later, you'll have to come to terms with your emotions. The sooner, the better...."

Karen Toller Whittenburg has always been an insatiable reader. She even recalls getting into trouble in grade four for reading a book rather than working on her math. And she still wishes her mother had kept the numerous stories she wrote as a child. But a few years ago, Karen's creativity was rewarded when she sold her first book. Since then, thirteen more have been published and she says she's never happy unless she has a romance in the works.

Inspiration for *Only Yesterday* came when Karen visited Galveston Island, Texas— an ideally romantic setting for two people in love. Karen lives in Oklahoma with her husband and three children.

Books by Karen Toller Whittenburg

HARLEQUIN AMERICAN ROMANCE

197–SUMMER CHARADE
249–A MATCHED SET
294–PEPPERMINT KISSES

Don't miss any of our special offers. Write to us at the following address for information on our newest releases.

Harlequin Reader Service
901 Fuhrmann Blvd., P.O. Box 1397, Buffalo, NY 14240
Canadian address: P.O. Box 603,
Fort Erie, Ont. L2A 5X3

Only Yesterday

KAREN TOLLER WHITTENBURG

Harlequin Books

TORONTO • NEW YORK • LONDON
AMSTERDAM • PARIS • SYDNEY • HAMBURG
STOCKHOLM • ATHENS • TOKYO • MILAN

For Keith,
my brother and very first hero

Published June 1990

ISBN 0-373-25403-2

1

"WE'RE EXPERIENCING some minor turbulence. Please observe the No Smoking sign and remain in your seat." With a crackling, splintery sound, the overhead speaker shut off and the cautioning seat belt light blinked off, then on again.

Merry McLennan glanced toward the front of the plane where two flight attendants conferred, their blond curls almost identical in color and cut, their uniforms a bright contrast of orange and blue. They balanced gracefully, despite the rough, unsettling movements of the plane. There was something very wrong about this flight from Denver to Houston.

Merry turned her head toward the tiny window and stared at the billowy clouds below. On the ground, it might be gray and gloomy and raining, but at this altitude, there was a soft sunset sky, blue and pink and vivid, the color highlighting row upon row of pristine clouds.

And turbulence. There was that, too. The airplane bucked against an insistent wind, then leveled off. The blond attendants smiled in unison and bustled off. But Merry had flown enough in her twenty-six years to recognize the distress they were unable to conceal and she knew their over-bright smiles hid a major worry.

"Something's wrong." The whisper came from the person sitting directly behind Merry. The voice was softly feminine, threaded with doubt, but audible.

"It's the wind." The corresponding whisper was masculine and reassuring. "The captain said it was some minor turbulence. Nothing to worry about."

Merry couldn't help glancing at the man who sat beside her, to see if he'd heard the exchange, to see if he, too, was concerned. He was watching her . . . or perhaps he was merely trying to see past her through the window. She leaned back, allowing him room, and noted from beneath lowered lashes that he was not reassured by the view.

How did she know that? Was it the frown that slowly creased his forehead and crinkled lines of tension at the corners of his mouth? Or was it the question that darted across his face? He was attractive, with brown hair and eyes, a slender build complemented by wide shoulders and a broad chest. His clothing was casual—a short-sleeved sports shirt and khaki slacks—but there was a stern look about him as if the easy-going style masked a more somber purpose. Perhaps he owed his intellectual, enigmatic look to the dark-rimmed reading glasses he'd put on once the flight was in progress. Whatever the reason, the overall effect was pleasing.

She'd noticed him when he'd first boarded the plane and asked if the seat beside her was taken. She'd have preferred that the seat remain empty. At one time, she'd have purchased both seats in order to protect her privacy, but she'd learned a lot during the past eight years and she knew there were other, more effective ways to keep strangers from violating her solitude.

Her eyelids closed, then bounced open with the rough movement of the airplane. Startled, she looked straight into the man's eyes. Brown eyes . . . a rich, earthy brown. And in that split second he seemed to look past her composure to see the fear waiting inside her. A small tremor of awareness speeded up her already accelerated heart-beat.

Merry turned away. She recognized the sensation as physical attraction and knew the man felt it, too. She sensed, as well, that he wished to speak to her, but she kept her gaze pinned to the window and willed the momentary attraction to pass. It wasn't so odd, she thought, to experience a flicker of sexual chemistry in the midst of a turbulent flight. She was anxious and a helpless participant in whatever happened, so her subconscious reached out for a hero and found him, sitting beside her. It was a mind game, Merry decided. Nothing more. If the flight had been uneventful, she might not have noticed him at all.

THE PLANE HIT A POCKET of air, dropped, then bumped clumsily through. Lee's stomach lurched with the jerky motion and he fought the insistent logic that something was very wrong with the airplane. This was more than turbulence, more than a strong head wind. Even the pretty flight attendant taking drink orders two rows up the aisle looked harried, as if she could barely concentrate on whether the passengers wanted cola or soda, juice or a mixed drink.

Lee had been nervous for most of the past twenty-four hours, anyway. Ever since he'd caught sight of Emerry at the Denver airport. He'd recognized her at once although she bore only a slight resemblance to the image he'd committed to memory. Her hair was the same—ebony, thick and satiny as a December midnight—her eyes as blue as a country morning, and her skin as smooth as porcelain.

Yet she wasn't as strikingly beautiful as the young model whose pictures adorned both his office and his memory. It was as if an artist had taken a brush and soft-ened her youthful features, blending and toning until the vivid contrasts of her appearance were shaded in pastels and subtle tones. She still carried herself like a model, straight, tall and purposeful, but there was maturity in her face and figure, a look of confidence and content-ment that Lee found more alluring than the cool beauty in her photographs.

Getting the seat beside her had been a lucky break, or so he'd thought. But she'd done little more than glance in his direction during the entire flight and he, who generally had little difficulty in initiating conversation, felt as tongue-tied as a young boy. He had dozens of questions to ask her and yet, the first words of introduc-tion died in his throat.

A popping, sputtering noise crackled just beyond the cushioned interior of the plane. Lee turned, as did every other passenger, toward the right-wing windows. A murmur of alarm ran through the conversational hum and gradually subsided as one of the flight attendants offered a soothing explanation over the intercom. At least, Lee supposed it was meant to soothe. He couldn't believe anyone had been convinced. When he looked back, he encountered the same disbelief in Emerry's eyes.

Such blue eyes. Familiar to him in every detail and yet not familiar at all. They were shadowed now with ques-tions and doubts and dread, and he wondered if she were as coolly sophisticated as she appeared. It was hard to stay cool about anything in this situation. He didn't like the feel of it and wished he hadn't been quite so quick about following up the anonymous phone call he'd re-ceived. But he'd had to meet Emerry. He'd had to take the chance that the call was for real, that she would be on this plane. He'd thrown a few things into a suitcase, packed a briefcase with notes and research, and caught the first flight out of LA International to Denver.

Luckily, he had no commitments to break, no responsibility except to himself and his dissertation. For the past few months, he'd been living in his parents' beach home, while his parents traveled the country in an RV. He'd tried to juggle his job as a counselor at a private medical clinic with the demanding requirements for his doctoral studies, but finally had turned in his resignation. Fortunately, he'd saved enough money to supplement the small trust fund his grandfather had set aside for his college education. Lee appreciated being able to pursue his degree without financial worry. He'd had enough worry in gathering information for his study. But now, at last, realization of his goal was close. So close.

The overhead speaker clicked, buzzed and went quiet. Lee glanced up, as did Emerry. He felt her tension whisper to his, felt his own apprehension collide with Emerry's as the speaker rasped a second time. "Ladies and gentlemen, we are experiencing some difficulty with one of the engines. It is *not*, I repeat, *not* a life-threatening situation. However, as a precautionary measure, we are going to land at Amarillo. The delay should be no more than a half hour. We are now at—" a pause came, filled with a heavy, pulsing silence "—eighteen thousand feet and will be making our unscheduled stop at Amarillo's international airport in approximately fifteen minutes. Please remain in your seats and observe the No Smoking sign." Static filled the air and then the pilot spoke again. "This is a *minor* problem. There is no immediate danger."

The speaker clicked off. The plane bumped into a rough descent and tension inside the cabin thickened like an evening fog. *No immediate danger.* Merry wondered what that meant. Immediate danger as opposed to what? Danger at nine thousand feet? Or less?

She studied the white-capped clouds, trying to temper her rising concern with logic. Airlines had signals, their own individual distress codes. Three bell tones or any combination of tones would give the attendants notice of impending disaster and they would take action. What action, Merry didn't know, but as long as the pilot had time to use the intercom, she supposed the plane wasn't falling apart.

However she decided that was little consolation. Something was not as it should be. Fear crept like a high fever through the narrow cabin. The attendants exchanged concerned glances even as they reassured the passengers. Merry wished she had remembered to bring Taggert's latest book on acutherapy and then realized how foolish the thought was. If the plane was about to crash, why would she want to spend the harrowing minutes before impact trying to read about a questionable treatment method in physical therapy?

To keep from worrying about Molly. To keep from being terrified of what would happen to Molly. Merry shifted uncomfortably in the seat, watching the clouds roll past the window in gray, smoky waves, knowing that fear had caught her, knowing there was nothing she could do at this point to protect her daughter. Merry couldn't bear the thought of not being there to see Molly grow up. How could the plane crash, how could she crash with it, when she had someone so precious depending on her to survive?

No, Molly would never forgive her if she died in a plane crash, Merry thought. It was just the two of them. Molly's father had been ill when his daughter was born and he'd died just two months later. Merry had known it was coming and still the loss had been devastating. But she'd had Molly and in the three years since Ian's death, they'd become quite a team. This was the first time they'd been apart for more than a few hours. The plane couldn't crash, Merry told herself. Fate wouldn't be so cruel. Merry wouldn't even allow herself to think about what would happen if Molly had to go to live with her grand-mother, Merry's mother.

A tone chimed once, then again, then . . . again. The attendants moved calmly, but quickly out of the aisles to strap themselves into their assigned seats. The atmo-sphere inside the cabin assumed a personality all its own. Foreboding rippled through the passengers. Somewhere in the back of the plane there was strained laughter. A panicked shout. The low hum of voices talking, pray-ing. A baby began to cry as the air pressure pushed against sensitive eardrums.

The plane was going too fast. It should have been slowing for the approach to the landing strip. Outside the window, clouds roiled up and away at an alarming, queasy rate. This was really happening, Merry realized as her stomach twisted in sudden, aching terror. Oh, Molly, she cried silently. I'm sorry. I'm so sorry.

The touch of a hand brought Merry's fingers curling instinctively into the grasp of the man beside her, ac-cepting the warm, comforting strength he offered. Merry turned to him, seeking an answer he couldn't begin to give. His eyes were clouded with concern, his jaw was a tight line of tension, but somehow—Merry couldn't im-agine why—he exuded a tranquility at odds with the sit-uation.

"My name is Lee," he said. "Lee Zurbaron." His voice wrapped her frantic thoughts in a husky calm.

"Merry," she answered, her voice thick and cluttered. "Merry McLennan."

"Mary?" A look of doubt furrowed his brow, a question implicit in his tone, as if he might have misunderstood her.

"M-e-r-r-y." She spelled it automatically, from years of dealing with misspellings. "As in Christmas."

"Merry, as in Christmas." He repeated her words slowly, rolling them on his tongue, etching them with a soft skepticism. "My favorite time of the year."

"I've never cared much for the holiday," Merry said only because she needed to talk and there was so little worth saying. "Even as a child, I never believed in Santa Claus." In all her life, she didn't think she'd ever confided that information. Why had she volunteered it *now*? Why was she talking about Christmas at all? Dear God! She was in the middle of a stormy sky, her only shelter a flawed, metal crate of modern technology. She might not live to hate Christmas for another year. And just when she'd begun to share her daughter's joy in the season. What if she didn't get to spend another Christmas with Molly? What if the plane did crash and this man, this Lee person, survived and told her mother what she'd said?

"My mother doesn't know I feel that way. She makes such a big deal about the holidays." Merry felt her voice catch, but couldn't prevent its revealing quaver on the last word.

Lee squeezed Merry's hand. "My mom, too. But I've always liked Christmas. It makes for some nice memories."

Merry was short on childhood memories, especially nice ones. She'd vowed that Molly would have all the pleasant remembrances, the special moments, that Merry herself, had missed. But now, facing the possibility that life might be shorter than she'd expected, Merry wondered if her daughter would even remember her.

"The plane is going to crash." Merry stated her thoughts quietly as she studied the strong lines and textures of the stranger's hand so securely fastened over hers.

"It looks like a definite possibility." Lee watched her face, pale with dread, but delicate and composed despite the situation. Her palm felt damp against his. Or maybe it was his palm that was sweating. A shaded smile lifted one corner of his mouth. He'd always heard that when a man met the woman of his dreams, he'd awaken with sweaty hands. If only Emerry were still just an image in his mind. If only he were safely tucked beneath the covers of his own comfortable bed, dreaming about sitting next to her, holding her hand. He'd been desperate to meet her, but he hadn't meant to put himself in danger to do so. What if he'd made a mistake? She'd said her name was Mary. Mary McLennan.

Merry, he corrected, and forced his mind to stop grasping at straws. She was Emerry Emilia Edwards, no matter what she called herself now. Dropping the first *E* in her name and using a different surname was a simple way of changing identities. Besides, he'd studied her pictures too long and too intently to be misled by a woman of similar appearance.

Beyond the window, through a misty rain, Lee caught a glimpse of runway lights, blinking and disappearing in the fog. He tightened his grip on her hand and hoped she wouldn't notice the lighted airstrip. It was better not to be braced or rigid if the plane didn't land smoothly.

"Where are you from, Merry? Denver? Houston?" Lee asked, wanting to distract her with small talk, thus protecting her in the only way he could.

"Austin." Her glance flicked to the window, then jerked back to him. "I, uh, live in Austin. I was at a . . . a conference in Denver and then—" her throat went dry; she swallowed "—umm, I'm on my way to Houston, well, Galveston, really, for a vacation. I'm meeting my. . . some friends at the Hotel Galvez." She didn't know why she balked at telling him about her daughter. Molly was staying with the Lesters, Merry's dearest and best friends in Austin. They were all to meet at the hotel the day after tomorrow. Merry hoped she could keep the appointment.

She realized she'd let her thoughts drift from the man beside her. . . Lee, she recalled, but his last name escaped her. Lee was talking to her and she hadn't been listening. Not closely, anyway. He'd mentioned California, she thought. And something about the beach, maybe. She couldn't retrieve the words, they flipped past her memory and out of reach. What difference did it make what he'd said? It was small talk, words to keep her from dwelling on the sensation of plummeting toward the ground. She looked out the window. His voice stopped and oddly, immediately, she missed the sound of it.

Turning back, she met his gaze. His dark eyes shared her fear. His firm handclasp weakened her terror and kept her calm. "Thank you," she whispered, hoping he understood.

The plane groaned and rolled to the left before buffeting itself aright. Air rushed through the resisting flaps and a throbbing roar flooded Merry's ears. Her heart pulsed a hard and fast rhythm of denial. *Everything will*

*be okay. This isn't happening. There is no real danger. It
will be all right.*

It didn't feel all right.

It felt dangerous, and she was scared for herself and
terrified for her child. Only Lee's handclasp was safe.
Only his steady breathing beside her was real. He would
survive, and as long as she held on to him, so would she.

The shriek of the engines grew unbearably loud, the
staticky whistle of wild, rushing air went higher and
faster…higher…faster. The plane touched down, jerked
up away from the runway, then lurched across the con-
crete strip like a drunk trying to walk a straight line. The
tail dipped downward, emitting a whine of scraping
metal; the nose flipped up, pushing Merry flat against the
seat, then bumping her forward as the airplane regained
a measure of balance. There was another lurch, as if the
wheels were grabbing for any support, searching for any
means of control. The lights went out, plunging the cabin
into an eerie darkness. In the next half second, the plane
dived, pushing Merry against the seat belt. They were
spinning, turning in a frenzied semicircle of arrested
speed. Then it was over.

The noise stopped and in the momentary hush, Merry
heard the beating of raindrops. The steady, rhythmic,
beautiful sound of rain. Someone, somewhere near, began to sob and then the panic began. "Get out!" A man
yelled. "There's smoke!"

"Fire!"

"The plane's on fire!"

"Get out!"

The flight attendants moved quickly and efficiently to
the exits, all the time trying to maintain control. "Please,"
they repeated in various tones, at different places,

"Please, remain calm. There's plenty of time. Don't panic."

Merry made no move to join the maddening crowd in their rush to the emergency exits. She sat, curiously unconcerned by this newest threat of fire. Lee held her hand and she was secure in the knowledge that he would not let her go. When he stood, she followed suit. They waited for the aisle to clear somewhat and she realized he was not much taller than she. Of course, she was wearing heels, but not high ones. Weren't rescuers supposed to be extraordinarily tall? She was five-nine, and he couldn't have been more than two inches taller, if that much. She was used to being at eye level with her colleagues. Dr. Walters, the head of the Burnstein Clinic, was quite a bit shorter than she, and Merry didn't give his stature a second thought. But Lee . . . Well, for some reason, she was surprised.

"I'm afraid we'll have to leave our luggage behind for now." Lee turned to her, his voice steady, his clasp strong and reassuring.

"It isn't important."

"No." He pressed her hand, sharing in one long look the knowledge that being alive was what was important. "Well, keep close. Here goes." He took a step forward, easing his way into the aisle and making room for her, as well.

Merry braced herself against the pull of the plane's downward slant and hoped the people in front of her would get out quickly and safely. She needed to remove herself from the frenzy of noise and distress. She liked things to be controlled. She liked to be in control. But here, squeezed between Lee and another passenger, there was nothing to do, except wait. "Do you think there is a fire? I can smell smoke."

"I imagine it's the odor of rubber tires. There are probably some sensational skid marks on the runway."

"Let me by!" A woman pushed forward from behind them, her voice a high-pitched measure of her anxiety. "Get out of the way. I've got to get out of here!" She all but climbed the seats in her hysteria and as she threw herself past them, Merry shrank into the sheltering angles of Lee's body. His arms came around her to provide a calm and secure haven. Breathless sensations flowed through her body and she was very much aware of the turmoil within herself.

Heat swept through her and she realized how good it felt to be close to Lee. A shifting, nameless emotion stirred in her stomach, teasing her with longings and desires she'd buried along with Ian. These feelings formed a tender trap, an illusion of safety and strength. Lee was her knight in shining armor at the moment, and she responded with a very feminine yearning to believe in heroes. It wasn't real, this attraction that had arisen through crisis. She knew it, understood it, but still she stayed in his arms, stubbornly clinging to his hand no matter how awkward the contact became.

"Now there's a lady who knows what she wants." Lee made reference to the hysterical woman who now was pushing her way to the emergency exit. His voice was a throaty rumble against Merry, his humor a flicker of light in the dark drama surrounding them. "I hope she doesn't hurt herself or someone else."

Merry nodded and wished silently for the waiting to end. She understood the woman's panic and knew her own was just restrained by early training. *Smile. Stand up straight. Chin up. Shoulders back. Don't be a baby. You can do it.* All the voices of her past whispered through her mind, advising her that outward appearance was all-important. If you look calm, other people perceive you as calm and you become calm. And you photograph better. Merry had learned the lesson well.

So why was she huddling—there was really no other word for it—against a stranger? Why wasn't she calm and in control of her racing pulse? Why did he continue to hold her so protectively, as if he understood the depths of her fear, as if he saw far more of her emotion than she had let him see?

Then, almost unexpectedly, the aisle in front of her cleared. Somehow the evacuation became smooth and orderly as one after another, the passengers slid down the emergency chute to the rescue crews below. The woman who had created such a furor only moments before twisted her ankle as she reached the runway. Merry watched over the shoulders of the remaining passengers in front of her as the woman was carried toward a first-aid vehicle.

"You were right," Merry said to Lee. "She hurt herself."

"Make sure nothing like that happens to you," he said. "We've come too far to risk getting hurt at this stage." His breath warmed her temple, stirring a strand of her hair and a deep restlessness inside her. "Be careful, Merry-as-in-Christmas. I've waited a long time to find you."

No man had spoken to her with such care in a long time. It was at once a protective comment and a seductive challenge. She didn't know what to say, how to act, where to look. The past fifteen minutes had been fraught with emotion. She had to believe he was only acting under the influence of the stress . . . as was she.

Without a word, she bent and slipped off her shoes. Holding them together in one hand, she sat at the top of the chute, listened to the flight attendant's instructions and pushed away from the plane to slide to safety. A fireman, dressed in a silver, flameproof suit, grabbed her by the arms and pulled her to her feet. Another rescue worker guided her away from the crippled airplane to an area where other passengers stood waiting. Merry glanced back just in time to see Lee reach the ground and flash a smile of relief at a fireman.

Lee had been afraid, too. She'd known that, of course. But at that moment, she realized how much she had depended on his belief that everything would be all right, on his courage in the ugly face of danger. Now he was just happy to be safe, to be alive. She watched as he paused, his eyes scanning the crowded runway to find her. When his smile settled on her, a sense of tranquility, of calm in the midst of a storm, folded over her. The rain was a steady drizzle, but she didn't feel the dampness or the chilly wind. She knew only that circumstances had taken her from her neat, orderly world and placed her here, on a crowded runway, among perfect strangers.

Lee reached her side, asked if she was all right and put his arm around her shoulder in a gesture as friendly as it was masculine. Merry would never have allowed it...in another place, another time. But the near tragedy had stripped away her disillusionment with life and she was simply glad to be alive and to have someone with whom to share the feeling. Lee, whose last name she couldn't remember, was a stranger, but she felt incredibly close to him, as if she'd known him all her life. She had placed her trust in him the moment he'd taken hold of her hand and she wasn't yet ready to sever that bond.

Trust was, after all, a relative term.

2

A CURIOUS SORT of camaraderie developed among the passengers of the crippled airplane. Merry didn't know quite how or when the rapport established itself, but there was no mistaking the unity of the group now gathered in the airport lobby. They were awaiting transportation to a nearby hotel—all accommodations considerately provided by the airline—and restless chatter bounced from person to person.

"Do you think they'll send a limo?"

"Naw, it'll probably be a van. Most of these hotels have vans, you know. More practical."

"I don't understand how those people could get right back on another airplane after what happened. My family is driving up tomorrow to get me. The last thing I want to do is fly."

"I'm not worried about flying. I just want to relax a bit and get a good night's sleep before I put on another seat belt."

The conversations continued, but Merry stepped out of the close-knit circle. Her first inclination had been to take the airline's offer of another flight, forget about the scheduled vacation in Galveston and fly home to Molly. But a phone call had changed her mind. Janie Lester had convinced Merry that rest and recreation were more necessary now than ever before. "The last thing you needed was another emergency," Janie had said. "Stay there tonight. Go on to Galveston tomorrow. We'll be

there the next day. Use the time in between to relax. You'll
need all the energy you can get to vacation with your
Molly. She's so excited she can barely stand still. Here,
talk to her a minute."

The sound of her daughter's voice provided Merry
with the added incentive to leave her vacation plans intact. Molly was thrilled to talk to her mother, thrilled to
be spending the week with the Lesters and their daughters, Carol and Katy, thrilled to be going to "Gavston,"
and couldn't wait to see the ocean waves. She giggled and
chattered until Merry's smile turned as soft as ice cream.
When the conversation was over, Merry ached to hug her
daughter, but was resigned to sticking with her original
plans, except that she would delay her arrival in Galveston until the next day. She had no reason or desire to
arrive at her destination in the middle of the night.

So now, she stood alone, waiting to be taken to the
hotel, waiting to release her lingering tension in a warm
bath and a comfortable bed. There was such relief in
being on solid ground, she felt restless. When she saw Lee
put down the receiver of a public telephone on the other
side of the lobby, a feeling of eagerness cut through her.
This surprised her, intrigued her. Was it because of the
experience they'd shared? Or could it be something else?

She took a step toward him. He smiled when he saw
her and a steady warmth circled in her stomach. How
long had it been since a man had excited her with a look?
In fact, when was the last time she'd responded to a man,
whether he'd looked at her or not? She couldn't answer
either question and told herself she was experiencing the
aftereffects of intense emotion. It wasn't anything personal. *How could it be?*

She watched as he walked toward her with a stride that
carried a determination and confidence all its own. His

hair picked up the glint of overhead lights and looked lighter than it had on the plane. It wasn't blond, but it wasn't quite brown, either. She wondered if it bleached out in the summer sun and darkened in the winter months. Hadn't he said something about living on the beach?

Lee slowed down as he approached Merry. The slightest curve of her lips greeted him. There was a soft welcome in her eyes. He'd found her. After two years of research and a solid year of searching, he'd actually found her. Emerry Emilia Edwards stood not fifteen feet away, smiling at him, and he realized he'd made a mistake. Sitting beside her on the plane, he'd thought he could introduce himself casually, tell her about his dissertation, about his studies of child stars and the effects of fame on their later lives. He'd even worked out a plausible explanation of how he'd found out she'd be on that particular flight. Not precisely the truth, but close enough. And now, suddenly, he knew he'd made a tactical error.

It was going to be a little awkward now to tell her he was a psychologist who'd followed a blind lead in order to find her and write about her past. A past she'd obviously gone to great pains to put behind her. He should have introduced himself earlier, but how could he have known the plane would develop a hydraulics problem? His efforts to comfort her and himself had been sincere. But now he was cast in the role of rescuer and he'd lost the opportunity of simply introducing himself and telling her about his intent.

"Did your call go through this time?" she asked as he stopped beside her.

"Yes. No problems." What would she say if she knew he'd just phoned the Hotel Galvez for reservations to begin the following day? He hoped to wrangle an invitation from her before the night was over, but he was determined to go with her to Galveston one way or the other. "Did you get in touch with your friends?"

"Yes. My daughter's staying with them and it was good to hear her voice."

"You have a daughter?"

Merry nodded. "Molly is three. This is the first time we'll be apart for more than a day and I, well, I guess I was anxious to rush to the phone and make sure she was all right." She pushed back a strand of ebony hair. "That sounds silly, I guess, but she has no one else and I was afraid that if something happened to the plane, if I didn't get home to her..." The explanation trailed into nothing and she pressed her lips together, as if she wished she hadn't spoken at all.

"Her father?"

"He died."

"How tragic for you."

Merry gave no acknowledgement of his sympathy and Lee knew she regretted the meager confidences she'd shared. "I'm surprised you decided to stay over," she said. "Somehow, when the airline official announced our alternatives, I thought you'd be the first one in line for the next flight out."

Lee smiled easily, glad she hadn't noticed that he'd waited to find out her plans before making his own decision. If she'd chosen to fly on to Houston, he would have opted for that, too. "Not me. I've never put much faith in the old adage that if you get thrown off a horse, you should get back on at the first opportunity. After this afternoon's experience, I'm convinced it doesn't apply to airplanes and collapsed hydraulics systems and me. In fact, I came within a whisper of opting for the Trail-

Master Bus ticket . . . and I hate traveling by bus across town, much less across Texas."

"It's good to know I wasn't the only coward."

"Look at this group. You're not the only one who didn't feel like flying again tonight."

It was obvious, of course, but Merry hadn't really associated herself with the rest of the passengers. She had stayed with Lee through the evacuation of the plane, through the trip to the terminal, through the long minutes while they'd waited to learn what had gone wrong and what would happen next. Lee was her link to the others and to the reality of the unreal situation in which she found herself. It wasn't like her to depend upon someone else, especially a stranger. But Lee didn't seem like a stranger. He had provided strength when she'd been unable to supply her own and even now, with the danger past, she felt the solid, simple power he possessed . . . and something inside her clung to it.

"Attention! May I have your attention?" The airline official who earlier had offered sincere apologies and regrets on behalf of the airline came through the front doors of the airport and clapped his hands above the noise. "The vans are here for those of you who are going to the hotel. Everything has been arranged. You are guests of the airline and we want you to be as comfortable as possible."

The crowd began to disperse. People moved forward. Some held back, perhaps unsure of leaving the security of the building for the vehicles outside. Merry had no such compunction. She wanted nothing more than to reach the hotel. She felt out of sync, as if the turbulent movements of the plane had disturbed her perspective and tossed her emotions into an unrecognizable jumble.

Lee reached for her suitcase, but Merry's hand closed on the handle a split second before his fingers curved over hers. Unexpected, inexplicable awareness tingled up her arm, wrapped around her chest, teased her with peppery flickers of heat. Her gaze flew to his for one long, shivering instant. "I can manage this," she said, and then had to clear her voice of an irritating breathiness. "Thanks, but you have your hands full with your own luggage."

His hand lingered briefly on hers before he moved to pick up the two bags at his feet. Merry pulled the strap of her carry-on luggage across her shoulder, picked up the Pullman case, and started toward the exit, telling herself there were a hundred plausible explanations for the attraction she was feeling. Her subconscious was hard at work to convince her that Lee—she still didn't remember his last name—was a modern-day hero, a man who could and would save her from airplane crashes and other disasters, sweep her off her feet and carry her away to a fantasy land of happily-ever-afters. And the ridiculous part was that she didn't even know anything about him.

Well, that wasn't entirely true, she decided a few minutes later when she was scrunched between Lee and another man on the narrow back seat of an eleven-passenger van. If she were honest, she had to admit that she did know a few things about him. He was a sensitive man . . . on the plane, when she'd been so afraid, hadn't he taken her hand without any kind of blustery, emotional explanations? He possessed self-confidence . . . witness the way he'd bridged the gap of tension and fear by stating his name in that calm, sandpapery voice. He didn't panic, not even in the throes of a very real danger. And he had gentle eyes, warm and caring.

And seductive. Darkly seductive.

She didn't know where that thought had come from. It wasn't as if she wanted...as if she'd imagined... being in his arms, tasting the sensual fullness of his lips— an image which appeared uninvited in her mind and was more disturbing than the mere thought of his seductive eyes. She pushed both image and thought aside. Although she knew a little more about him than she'd expected, that was no reason to give way to foolish fantasies. Regardless of the circumstances.

"So, where are you all from?" The driver of the van peered in the rearview mirror, curiosity crinkling around the corners of his eyes. "Guess ya didn't think you'd be staying the night in Amarillo, did ya?"

A general ripple of laughter greeted his overtures, and Merry was struck again by the common bond that had somehow come into existence among this group of travelers. She observed it, felt it and yet couldn't become a part of it.

At moments like this, she wished she were a less private person. There was an atmosphere of jocularity aboard the van, as if each individual shared the same glad sense of having been rescued, of getting a second chance to live. Merry wanted to be a part of it, but simply didn't know how.

"I'm from Denver," someone in the front said. "I was flying to Houston to visit my sister."

"My wife and I have been skiing," said a young man who was sitting next to a rosy-cheeked young woman. "We live in Friendswood."

"Really?" It was the driver again. "I have a cousin who lives there. Nice place."

"Texas is a nice place." A man two seats away spoke up. "I'm from Baytown and I love this state."

Several people in the van agreed, repeating the sentiment with an almost fierce loyalty. There was an underlying edge of tension running beneath the high spirits of this group, Merry realized. If she were any judge, she'd say they were all walking a fine line of emotional control.

Out of the corner of her eye, Merry noticed that Lee had withdrawn a bit. He was still smiling, but she had the idea that he, too, recognized the subtleties of stress. She wanted to touch him, reach for his hand, maintain the fragile thread of contact between them. She almost did. But something . . . inner caution, maybe . . . stopped her. This interdependent relationship she had allowed to develop could not continue. It wasn't real.

"Anyone from Austin?" someone asked and Merry was pulled back to the group's conversation.

"I am," she said.

The man on her left looked at her with interest. "Do you know Tommy Webster? He has a hardware store there."

Merry smiled politely, even though she wished she hadn't opened herself up to questions, no matter how innocuous. "No," she answered. "It's a large city."

"Yes." The man leaned forward, his gaze narrowing. "Say, you look familiar. Don't I know you from somewhere?"

Merry's heart froze, but her self-protection system kicked into gear. "I don't think so." Her voice made a soft, laughing denial. "People are always saying that to me. I guess I have an all-American face."

"No, really," the man persisted. "You look like someone I've seen . . ." His words trailed into a thoughtful silence, but Merry knew he was very close to recalling the name, Emerry Edwards. It had happened to her before. Someone would say, "Hey, aren't you the Sunshine girl? Didn't you used to be on TV?" But instead of becoming easier to deny, it was getting harder each time. Harder, because she wanted so much to forget. Harder, because her past was like a shadow, always so close it startled her. She prepared, now, to deny it once again.

"What's the temperature here tonight?" Lee asked the driver. "I'm from California, and it feels extremely warm to me."

The driver laughed a smug, Texas-is-for-real-men kind of laugh. "Yeah," he said. "You're gonna find it's pretty hot in Amarillo. No ocean breezes around here. Why, I've seen rain change into steam in midair. Right in the city limits."

The conversation in the van turned to weather and tall Texas tales. Merry breathed a grateful sigh as the man beside her let himself get distracted. Under a fold of her summer skirt, Lee's hand moved against hers and gave her knuckles a squeeze, almost as if he knew of her momentary distress. He couldn't know, of course, but she felt uneasy somehow. Maybe because Lee had rescued her again . . . and she already felt too close to him. She moved her hand safely onto her lap.

Lee noted her retreat and told himself to stop acting the hero. Why hadn't he let the man continue his questioning? How easy it would have been to let someone else say, "You're Emerry Edwards, aren't you? You were the Sunshine girl. You advertised skin-care lotions for Hamil and Harrison. I watched you grow up on television. I always enjoyed those commercials. What ever happened to you?" Lee rubbed the bridge of his nose, unconsciously arching his wrist out of the way of the glasses he wasn't wearing. He'd taken them off before exiting the plane, but he was so accustomed to having them on, it was a reflex action to accommodate the thin, tortoiseshell frame. Still, corrective lenses or no, he knew Merry McLennan *was* Emerry Edwards. So why hadn't he taken the opportunity just now to guide the conversation, to let the other man lay the groundwork for him?

Because he'd sensed Merry's distress and, like an idiot, had rushed to the rescue. He didn't generally make two mistakes in the same day, especially not when it came to his research. And Emerry or Merry was his research. True, she wasn't like the other child stars he'd studied. She was different, running from her past success rather than clinging to it. But the feelings he was experiencing had little to do with her past. And a lot more to do with the haunting loveliness of her violet-blue eyes. He really could not afford a personal interest in her.

She shifted beside him, her arm brushed his and Lee tensed with the touch. A subtle need made itself known in the pit of his stomach and his thoughts took a broad leap in the direction of personal interest. With some difficulty, he brought them to heel and released a silent sigh of relief when the van pulled to a stop in front of a new-looking, multistoried hotel.

Welcome Texas Bluebelles, AAA Champs! proclaimed the marquee at the entrance of the parking area. Below that hung the Best of the West emblem of quality and a discreet Vacancy sign. Merry took in the surroundings with a studied glance as she waited her turn to step down from the van.

Once on solid ground, Merry resisted the impulse to wait for Lee and paused only long enough to get her bearings before she walked into the lobby. At the desk, she spoke to the clerk and began to fill in the registration card he handed her. She knew when Lee came to stand beside her, but she gave him no acknowledgement. Really, she thought, it was best to end this attraction—friendship, whatever it was—now before he rescued her a third time.

Lee realized a cool front had suddenly developed, but he told himself it was a natural reaction on Merry's part. Merry didn't want him—or anyone—to get too close. The idea scared her, he knew. So he would back off...for the moment, anyway. But he'd come too far and had too much at stake now to quit when he was so close to realizing his goal—*professional goal*. He qualified the thought as he reached for the registration form and began filling it in.

A hubbub of noisy activity erupted behind him and he turned to see what was going on. People clustered around a woman who was slipping quietly, quickly to the floor despite the bevy of hands that reached out to catch her.

"Help!" a man said in a voice that barely carried across the room. "She needs help."

"I think it's a heart attack," someone said.

"Heart attack," another voice echoed.

Lee turned, intending to ask the desk clerk to call for medical assistance, when he heard Merry take charge of the situation. "Get back. Give her room to breathe."

There was a startled silence and then the obedient shuffle of feet as everyone moved out of the way. Lee moved closer, gaining a view of Merry on her knees beside the woman, checking for pulse and respiration. Her movements were smooth, efficient, and skillful. Her hair swung forward, a veil of ebony satin across her cheek, in the instant before she impatiently caught it behind her ear. "She's fainted," Merry said. "That's all. It's a form of shock. Get those pillows off the sofa," she instructed a uniformed hotel employee who was hovering nearby.

"Shock?" A man—the woman's husband, Lee suspected, because of the worry etched into his face—questioned Merry as she placed the pillows under the woman's feet. "But how can she be suffering from shock now?"

"Psychogenic shock. A delayed reaction," Merry explained. "Don't you remember—one of the medical rescue workers told us to watch out for this kind of thing. It's not uncommon for someone to faint several hours after a near-tragic accident. And that's what's happened here. She's fainted."

"Are you a doctor?"

Merry shook her head, releasing the captured tendrils of hair from behind her ear. "I'm a physical therapist."

"Maybe we ought to call a doctor . . . just to be on the safe side."

"That's an excellent idea." Merry rose. "Keep her feet elevated slightly for the time being." She walked back to the registration desk and looked inquiringly at the clerk. "May I have a key now? I'd like to go to my room."

"Yes, ma'am." The young man jumped to attention, barely glancing at the registration card she pushed across the counter. "That was really something, ma'am. I didn't know physical therapists could do that kind of thing."

"Anyone could have done what I just did for that woman," Merry told him firmly. "Everyone ought to know enough first aid to react quickly. This wasn't a life-threatening emergency. But it might have been."

"It was quick thinking on your part, Merry." Lee felt she deserved commendation for her quick response. He admired both her ability and the calm she'd brought to a frantic situation. "I've taken a first-aid course, but the only thing I could think of was to call an ambulance."

One corner of her mouth twitched with a rueful slant. "This seems to be a night for rescues, doesn't it?"

"Yes," he said, wondering who was going to rescue him. He was drowning in emotions that had nothing to do with research. "Would you like me to rescue your luggage and carry it upstairs for you?"

"The bellman will do that," the desk clerk interjected, and Merry acknowledged him with a nod.

She hesitated, then extended her hand to Lee. "I guess we should say goodbye, now. I doubt we'll see each other tomorrow, so..."

Lee knew he was supposed to take the initiative, ease them through the amenities of a polite goodbye, but he had no intention of saying it. "I'll walk you to your room."

"No." She cut short his offer and he knew, somehow, that she was drowning, too. "I want to thank you, Lee, for..." Her voice quavered slightly, then firmed with control. "Thank you. And goodbye." She turned and walked to the elevator, head up, shoulders back, poised and confident, as if she were unaware of Lee's observation, as if she were undisturbed by that pragmatic farewell. Lee knew she was aware that he watched her. He knew she hadn't wanted to say goodbye, but she was protecting herself as, he suspected, she always protected herself. And the knowledge whetted his interest. Both professional *and* personal.

"Classy lookin', isn't she?" the desk clerk said. "But kinda cool, if you know what I mean."

Lee waited until Merry had stepped into the elevator and out of sight before he answered. "She's been through a stressful couple of hours. We all have." He picked up the pen absently, thinking that he wouldn't have described her as classy, although she undeniably was. And cool? Well, he could see where a young man, like the desk clerk, might be put off by Merry's poise. But Lee found her fascinating. Self-controlled, yes, but vulnerable. She was intriguing and he wouldn't be satisfied until he knew who she really was.

He completed the registration form and slid it across the countertop in exchange for a room key. In the lobby behind him, a general buzz of activity increased as the ambulance arrived and paramedics came through the doorway. Some of the airline passengers had moved to the desk and were registering there, but some stayed with the woman who had fainted, talking, sharing the common bond of their unusual circumstances.

Lee walked away from them and the day's events without a backward glance. He was going to shower, change clothes and relax for a few minutes, before he convinced Emerry to have dinner with him. Emerry Edwards, he thought. The Sunshine girl. The missing link in his study. And she was all wrapped up in a mysterious woman named Merry.

The elevator signaled its arrival with a low-pitched tone. Lee tapped his foot, impatient with the wait, eager to be with her again. Merry McLennan, he thought as he stepped inside the elevator and punched the button for his floor... and hers. Merry. As in Christmas.

3

THE ROOM WAS ADEQUATE, sea green and lonely. Merry stood at the window, missing Molly, wishing for the comfort of familiar things and comparing the gray, wet view to the dreary, dry decor of the hotel. She'd planned on soaking her tense muscles in the tub and going to bed, but had settled for a shower and a change of clothes, instead. It was too early for bed and she was too keyed up to sleep, anyway. Her stomach growled, reminding her of how long it had been since lunch, but she couldn't bring herself to go downstairs to the restaurant. The "group" would most likely be gathered there and, although she longed for company, she knew she would feel even lonelier in their midst.

It was Lee she thought of as she stared out the hotel room window. Lee, whose touch still warmed her hand, whose image filled her memory. She shivered, not knowing why. She felt distanced from herself, as if she had stepped off the plane and into the Land of Oz. Why else was she feeling isolated? Why else was she fantasizing about a man she barely knew? Silly. How could she be hungry for his companionship, the stimulating energy of his presence, when only a few hours ago she hadn't even known he existed? And how, *how*, could her body ache to be caught up close to his? How could she *need* to feel his arms around her when she hadn't needed a man . . . not like that . . . in years?

It didn't make sense, not even considering the raw state of her emotions after the harrowing events of the afternoon. It was a good thing she'd bid him a brusque goodbye.

Merry closed the drape with a shaky hand. Her feelings scared her. And yet, something in her wanted to reach out and grab them, explore them, find out if she was missing a whole sphere of emotion and happiness. She knew women who, upon meeting an attractive, interesting man, tossed caution to the wind and plunged into a relationship that lasted a day, or a week, or forever. How did they take that first reckless step into the unknown? She didn't know the answer, but tonight, for the first time, she had an insight as to why they did it. If Lee were here now . . .

Nothing would happen, she told herself. Trust didn't naturally come into play for her. From an early age she'd been conditioned to keep herself apart, never to allow anyone to glimpse the real person beneath the veneer.

"Shine, honey," Mary Evelyn Edwards, known as Emee to friends and foe alike, used to say. And Merry had learned to "shine." First for her mother, then for anyone who aimed a camera in her direction. She could go from dull-eyed weariness to a million-dollar smile in less time than it took the shutter to click. Her mother had trained her well and, in the process, had created a legacy of resentment and painful memories.

When she'd made the decision to leave modeling, Merry had fought her mother every step of the way. But at eighteen, she was legally free of Emee's parental authority and was determined to sever the ties to her childhood. So she'd walked away and stayed away. She'd signed over the bulk of her financial assets to Emee—the price of freedom was high—keeping only enough to pay for college as well as a modest amount of savings. It hadn't been easy, not by a long shot, but Merry had made it. She was, finally, free of Emerry Edwards and had a life she'd designed and planned for herself. Of course, she'd had Ian's help. Dear Ian, who had been there when she needed him...as a friend, as the father figure she'd never known and finally, eventually, as the husband she could depend upon. And now, she had Molly. Which was all the more reason to stay away from her past and to deny the truth whenever someone recognized her as the Sunshine girl. What Emee Edwards wouldn't give to get her hands on Molly, to put her in front of a camera, to be able to say again, "Shine, honey."

Merry sank onto the stiff cushions of the hotel room's only chair. It wasn't comfortable and she thought again about deserting her solitude for the restaurant downstairs, but she made no attempt to marry action to the thought. She didn't understand her mood or the strange restlessness in her body. After all, she'd just received another chance at living and all she could think about was how lonely she was.

What was Lee doing? she wondered, hating the weakness that made her think of his strength. Was he in his room or had he gone downstairs? She could join him. It would be a simple matter to ring the front desk, find out his room number and call him. But what would she say? "I'm lonely, so would you mind holding my hand?"

That wasn't her style, so Merry reached for the room-service menu instead. She'd order a sandwich and turn on the television. That ought to take her mind off food and her solitary condition.

Ten minutes later, she'd flipped through every channel offered on the television and had settled for a fuzzy, 1940s science fiction movie. It held her attention for the first five minutes, until the vegetation became the central character and started a rampage of carnivorous delight throughout the fictional town. Still, there was an element of suspense and she jumped when someone knocked on her door.

"Room service?" she asked as she went to the door. "That was fast."

"Room service," came the muffled reply, and she pulled open the door to find Lee standing there, wearing a smile and bearing a gift from which an appetizing aroma wafted. He'd showered, too; his hair glistened with a faint sheen of dampness. His clothes were casual, again—denim jeans, faded like a hazy summer sky, shrunk by repeated washings to mold masculine hips and thighs with low-riding, provocative comfort. A pullover shirt of light teal blue opened at the neck to reveal a cluster of golden-brown curls. Merry tried to ignore the annoying flicker of response in her fingertips, in other parts of her.

"I would have been here sooner, but the kitchen was kind of busy." He walked past her to enter the room. "I thought you might be hungry."

An equal mix of excitement and caution wound through her. She wanted him with her. Yet she was afraid of his closeness. Or maybe she was afraid because she was so very glad to see him. Whatever she felt, she didn't want him to know. "As a matter of fact, I've been waiting for room service to bring up the sandwich I ordered."

"This is better. Trust me."

Trust me. As if it were that simple, that easy. She closed the door and followed him to the center of the room.

"You should see the dining room downstairs," he said as he removed the linen cover from the tray. "Full to overflowing. People talking fast and furious about the silliest things. As if there was no tomorrow." He folded the linen and poured something from a silver carafe into a cup. It smelled appetizing and Merry moved closer. "I couldn't tell," he continued, "if it was our group from the airport or the Bluebelles, which I think is a softball team. Anyway, I decided to bring up a tray on the chance that you'd join me for dinner."

"I ordered from room service. It ought to be here in another ten or fifteen minutes."

"No need to starve in the meantime." Lee tugged at the table until it sat snugly between the bed and the chair, providing two places to sit. Merry crossed her arms at her waist, but hunger—whether for food or his company—kept her from making any protest at his blithe rearrangement of her room. Any protest would have lacked conviction. She was sure of it.

"It smells good," she offered tentatively.

Lee glanced up and smiled. With a gesture of his hand, he offered her the chair and Merry accepted. "I'm starving," she said as she settled in and tossed the napkin onto her lap. "What did you bring?"

"Salad, sirloin tips, grilled chicken breast, vegetables and dessert. Take your choice." He sank onto the edge of the bed and took the covers off the plates. Warm, delicious fragrances assailed her and Merry made short work of switching plates around to suit her taste.

"Is something wrong?" she asked a few minutes later. "Did you want the sirloin tips?"

His smile was slow and sure. "Do I look disappointed?"

"You keep eyeing my entree, even though you said I could choose."

"So I did, but I was sure you'd choose the chicken. Every woman I know seems to be on a no-red-meat, low-cholesterol diet. I just supposed you would be, too."

"I used to be on a very restricted diet, but I gave it up years ago. I'm still careful about what I eat, but I'm not compelled to count every calorie a dozen times."

"It's hard to believe you've ever had to watch your weight." With studied appreciation his dark gaze skimmed across her hips and down the long length of her legs. "In fact, you look like a model."

Her breath caught with the remark, but Merry took a slow swallow of her drink, telling herself it was an off-hand comment, nothing more, telling herself his sensual assessment could not be responsible for the unsettling increase in her heartbeat. "Oh, I'm a good ten pounds too heavy for modeling, but thanks for the compliment. I assume you meant it as a compliment?"

He didn't answer, but the curve of his lips told her he liked what he saw. Merry lowered her gaze. She didn't want him to look at her like that. It made her feel . . . she couldn't describe the sensations tumbling over and over inside her. It was as if she were spinning out of control. "The food's good," she said—because she felt she had to say something.

"Yes," he answered.

Merry put down her fork. "You haven't even touched it, Lee. Listen, do you want me to take the chicken?"

He glanced at the food on his plate as if he'd just realized it was there. "No, I prefer this. Really. I'm just having a little trouble concentrating. It's hard for me to believe I'm actually here with you."

"I know what you mean. Everything has an unreal quality about it, doesn't it? I guess that's only natural after coming so close to tragedy just a few hours ago."

"Very natural," he said, although he hadn't thought about the airplane incident for well over an hour. He couldn't believe he was finally face-to-face with Emerry Edwards. For so long now, she'd been a glossy image in a thousand photographs, a subject for study and speculation. He'd never thought she would be so . . . human. Or so delectably feminine.

Lee picked up the fork and stirred it once through the rice on his plate. How would he find out all he wished to know about this woman? How should he go about separating Emerry from Merry? "You know," he said casually—conversationally—"when I thought the plane was going to crash, I kept thinking about all the places I've never seen and all the things I haven't had a chance to do. Things like riding in a hot-air balloon, hiking through the Sierra Nevada, getting married, having kids. And then I thought about how everyone is supposed to be famous for fifteen minutes during their lifetime. I kept thinking I wasn't going to get my fifteen minutes of glory." He waited for her reaction, but the only change he could perceive was in the sudden shadowing of her blue eyes. "I guess," he continued, cloaking the deliberate words with a thoughtful tone, "everyone wants to be famous, even if it's only for a minute or two. Don't you think that's true?"

Merry pressed her napkin to her lips. "I think fame is grossly overrated. If people understood how . . ." She dropped the sentence there.

Lee waited a moment, then pursued it a bit further. "What about you, Merry? Have you spent your fifteen minutes basking in the spotlight?"

Fifteen minutes? She'd spent eighteen years of her life in that blinding, seductive glare. She almost told him, but she laughed away his question instead. "I don't care much for the spotlight, Lee. When the plane was going down, all I could think about was Molly and what would happen to her."

"That's understandable. Being the only living parent must mean a lot of extra worry. Do you get any help from Molly's grandparents?"

Merry reached for her water glass, shaking her head in answer to his question. "I never met Ian's parents. He was considerably older than I when we married and his parents had been dead for some time. As for my side of the family, I don't remember my own father."

"But your mother?" Lee asked. "Don't you see her?"

"All too often, I'm afraid. She lives in Denver and I saw her while I was there, although I usually don't visit her. Before Molly was born, Emee and I stayed as far from each other as possible...by mutual agreement. But since she became a grandmother, Emee finds an excuse to be in Austin every couple of months, and although she doesn't stay with me, she insists upon seeing her granddaughter while she's in town. I wish she'd limit her visits to Christmas and Molly's birthday, but she has me at a disadvantage. Molly thinks her 'Nina' is the grandest grandmother in the world, and I can't bring myself to deny Molly the contact with her only living grandparent, even though I'm not particularly comfortable with the arrangement." Merry patted her lips with the napkin. "The whole thing probably sounds odd to you, but my mother and I have an understanding."

Lee raised his glass to her. "So, basically, you're on your own with your daughter. What does that do to your social life?"

"It's pretty much limited to preschool programs and Disney movies. But I like it that way."

"What if you . . . met someone and fell in love?" Lee didn't know why he'd asked the question. It had nothing to do with what he wanted to know about her. And yet, it had everything to do with it.

"That's not going to happen."

"How can you be sure?"

Merry matched his gaze. "I don't believe in love or happy ever after, Lee. Not for me."

"Why not?"

Her lips tipped in a Mona Lisa smile and he knew she wouldn't answer. He tried several times as they ate to guide the conversation to her past, but each time Merry either changed the subject or simply didn't reply to his questions. She revealed little about herself and showed a rather unflattering disinterest in his life. Oh, she asked about California and she made a couple of inquiries regarding his home, but she didn't ask the usual questions that crop up between new acquaintances.

She avoided personal comments and it finally occurred to Lee that she felt safer in not learning too much about him. Merry maintained her privacy by keeping people at a distance. She obviously didn't want him, or anyone, to get too close.

His observation strengthened during dinner and was firmly set by the time they'd finished eating. Although she conversed easily, he recognized the subtle tension in her movements and knew she was both intrigued and frightened by the attraction that sizzled between them at odd moments—when their eyes met and held or when his knee accidentally brushed against hers under the table. He knew she was vulnerable to the attraction no matter how hard she tried to disguise it. And against every professional instinct, every logic, he knew he was vulnerable, too.

"The clinic where I work," Merry told him over the last few swallows of her coffee, "is a rehabilitation facility. I like being able to work with a patient over a period of several weeks or months, helping them reach as full a recovery as possible."

Lee nodded and decided to make one last attempt to probe into her past. "Did you always want to be a physical therapist?"

Merry stared into her cup for a moment. "When I started college, I had no idea what I wanted. I only knew what I didn't want."

"Which was?"

She shook her head and put the cup down on the tray with finality. "Thanks for sharing your dinner with me, Lee. I don't know what I'll do with the sandwich I ordered from room service."

"By the time it gets here, you may be hungry again."

She laughed and leaned back in the chair. "I'm glad you were on that plane today, Lee."

He opened his mouth to tell her his presence had been no accident, but the words refused to come. She looked relaxed and alluring sitting there across from him, her olive-green skirt draped loosely against a slender thigh, her print blouse open to expose a throat of soft hollows and satin skin. Her lips curved in a sensual smile that created a low ache in his stomach. He had seen that smile before. He had studied photographs of her that revealed far more of her sleek, streamlined body than he could see now. But the smile, the pictures . . . that had been someone else. Emerry. A young woman on the brink of self-awareness, someone he could study dispassionately. The woman before him now was Merry and he was feeling far from dispassionate. She was mature, womanly, seductive, and yet somehow innocent in a way he didn't think Emerry had ever been. As a psychologist he knew the impression could not be true, but a streak of purely male intuition insisted that it was.

"I'm glad I was on the plane, too, Merry," he said and knew he'd better get off of her bed and out of her room before he completely lost perspective. "I should let you get some rest. It's been a harrowing day."

Merry stood when he did, gracefully unwinding from the chair. "You don't have to leave yet. It's not so very late—"

A knock at the door punctuated her protest. "Room service," a voice called from the hallway.

With a flip of her hand, Merry waved Lee back to his seat and answered the door. Lee watched her, listening to the murmur of her voice as she spoke with the bellhop, hearing the lilt in her tone, recognizing a husky thread of tension that matched the pressure building inside him. If he didn't get out of here soon, he thought, he was going to do something unprofessional and foolish. Something like kissing her.

He stood up as Merry walked back into the room with a tray in her hand. He would say good-night to her and leave. A simple, friendly good-night. When he'd regained a professional distance, he'd approach her again. He just needed a little time.

Setting the tray on the dresser, Merry offered him a rueful smile. "Would you like a sandwich?"

"Thanks, but I don't know where I'd put it. Besides, I really should be leaving." He took a decisive step toward the door and stopped to say his good-night. A mistake, he realized, the moment he was face-to-face with her, close enough to touch her, near enough to smell the clean, sunshine scent of her. He saw a flicker of anxiety in her eyes and knew she was dreading being alone again.

"Of course," she said. "You must be as tired as I am."

"Yes." In fact, he wasn't tired. Every nerve in his body sparked with a sensual energy. He made no move to leave, just stood there looking at her, wondering why he felt so protective and so helpless to resist his attraction to her. He knew he was not going to leave her tonight.

Glancing down, Merry sent her hands deep into the side pockets of her skirt and tried to reason with her sudden anxiety. She felt foolishly distressed at his leaving. Yet she'd been alone most of her life. Why was it such an intimidating proposition now? Was it being alone that worried her? Or was it not being with Lee? "Well," she said. "Thanks again. I'll probably see you tomorrow."

"We're on the same flight to Houston."

"Oh." A suffocating tension pressed against her lungs as she raised her eyes to his. "That's right." When his dark gaze dropped to her mouth for a heart-stopping moment, she grew weak, longing to feel his lips on hers. She'd never wanted to be kissed so badly. She'd never before experienced any of the tumultuous emotions whipping through her at this moment. She should tell him to go. Right now. Before she begged him to stay. No, she couldn't. Oh, but the look in his eyes, the soft temptation of his lips . . .

A heart beat loudly in the stillness, pulsing rhythmically in a desperate cadence. The sound grew faster, wilder. It was coming from her, Merry realized. Her heart, thundering like a wild and fierce storm, so real, so . . . audible. Did he hear it? Her tongue darted out to moisten lips that parted invitingly. He bent toward her.

And then she heard a scream. Muffled and distant, the scream came again and again. Lee's mouth, so close to her, tightened with a wry smile. "Sounds like the alien's winning." He glanced at the television. "I think the potted palm just devoured Las Vegas. My guess is he'll hit the Alka Seltzer plant next."

Breathing hard, as if she'd run a seven-minute mile, Merry spun toward the television, realizing it had been on ever since Lee's arrival. She'd been unaware of the background noise until the movie score blended with her own frenetic heartbeat. How embarrassing. She wasn't usually so . . . so oblivious to what was going on around her. She fought for control as she snapped off the science fiction film and turned to Lee. "I'm sorry, Lee. I forgot that was on. I usually don't—" She stopped, realizing he was still staring at the screen. "Did you want to see the end of the movie? I can turn it back on if you like."

"Leave it off," Lee said. His eyes centered on her mouth and moved slowly upward to her eyes. "I didn't realize the set was on until the music picked up that pulsating rhythm. I was beginning to think I'd have to apologize for my overly zealous heartbeat."

"Me, too," she said before she thought. And then, too, without thinking, she stepped closer, drawn by a feeling she dimly recognized and couldn't seem to resist. "We must still be feeling the effects of this afternoon's trauma."

Lee took her in his arms and gently, relentlessly pulled her against his strong, hard body. "That's as good an excuse as any," he said as his mouth laid claim to hers. There was nothing tentative about that first, scintillating touch. His lips opened warm and moist and demanding over hers and Merry spun in slow, delicate circles of pleasure. Her hands played across the width of his chest, rising and falling with the uneven pattern of his breathing, touching and testing the texture of his skin beneath the cotton shirt he wore. His lips left hers for the space of one ragged breath and then returned for more.

Merry groped through the spiral of sensations to find a glimmer of sanity. She couldn't remember ever responding so intensely to a kiss. She knew she'd never before let a man get so close to her, not in three hours...not in three years.

Something had happened in that plane this afternoon. Lee had come to her rescue and like the women she'd observed and judged reckless, she'd accepted—no, *invited* this embrace. Maybe subconsciously she wanted a hero. Or maybe it was the fire of an elemental attraction that kept her clutching his broad shoulders, clinging to the sweet passion of his kiss.

Merry could barely think. All she knew was his touch and a desperate sense of being part of a world she didn't recognize.

"Wait . . ." She drew back to whisper. "I can't even remember your name."

"Neither can I. But it will come back to me in a minute." He captured her lips again, tasting, teasing, courting her tongue with the tip of his. His hands curved in at her waist, pulling her close . . . closer than she'd thought possible. His name didn't matter, she decided, as she drifted into the hazy enchantment. Her name didn't matter, either. Only the sparkling sensations mattered, the beautiful, confusing, compelling sensation of floating on wave after wave of pure delight.

When the kiss ended in a series of soft, sipping, reluctant caresses and he moved his arms from around her, she was suddenly cold . . . until he took her hands in his and she was, once again, warm. So warm.

"Lee," she whispered, grasping for any thought that made sense. "Your name is Lee, but I forgot the last part."

"Zurbaron. William Lee Zurbaron."

Drawing a long breath, Merry nodded and took a small step away from him. She needed to pull her hands away, too, but she couldn't. "Does anyone call you Willie? Molly has an imaginary friend named Willie."

Lee's mouth slanted in a crooked smile. "My mother sometimes calls me Will. You know how mothers are."

"Yes." Merry watched the curve of his lips and lost the slim thread of conversation. A throbbing silence slipped in, like an unwelcome guest. Lee held her gaze for long, limitless minutes in which she could not look away. Swept by forces out of her control, she knew that if Lee kissed her again, she might agree to anything, regardless of logic, regardless of the cost.

"Let me stay with you, Merry."

His eyes were so dark she thought there must be a thousand secrets hidden behind them, but then his words penetrated. "What?"

"Let me stay with you tonight."

"No." It was more than a protest. She didn't want the evening to end like this. She'd believed Lee was different—a hero. Why couldn't he have left her that one illusion? "No, Lee. I'm not—I don't go in for casual sex. You really have no right to ask that."

"Merry..." His handclasp tightened on her fingers, guarding against any move she might make to pull away. "When the light goes out and the room goes dark tonight, I don't want to be alone. I thought maybe you felt the same way. I meant nothing more than that. It's just . . . well, hell, it's a lonely world and I need someone to hold my hand for a few hours. That's all I'm asking."

All? She couldn't believe him. Surely he wanted more than to just hold her hand. Why was she bothering to consider his suggestion? Because he was...someone she trusted. She knew it was true, even as the thought took root and flowered in her mind. She trusted Lee. But how? How did she know he was telling the truth and offering just a hedge against loneliness?

She knew. Somehow, her heart believed him. It had been a strange day. Maybe tomorrow she would shudder at the risk she was taking, but tonight... Well, tonight, it made perfect sense to invite this man to sleep with her, to share the long night together, close, comforted.

"All right, Lee."

His fingers squeezed hers with a promise as enigmatic as his smile. Merry thought for a moment he was going to say something, but instead he moved to the bed and scooted the table and chair back into their original positions. As she watched, Merry wondered if she shouldn't change her mind, tell him to leave. Was she crazy to have agreed to let him stay?

Her heart fluttered at her indecision, but no request for him to leave passed her lips. The words froze on her tongue and melted beneath the memory of his kiss. She wouldn't let him kiss her again, she decided. She wouldn't take that risk. With that compromise made, she walked to the bed and pulled back the covers, feeling incredibly self-conscious as she made the intimate preparations. This wasn't such a good idea, she thought, and the cycle of doubt began again.

But Lee erased her dilemma when he got into bed, fully clothed, and pulled her down beside him. "Relax," he said as he reached to turn off the light. "Pretend I'm your imaginary friend. We'll both sleep better."

Merry smiled in the darkness. Safe, she thought. She was safe. "Goodnight, Willie."

She heard the soft thud as his shoes hit the carpet and then there was nothing except the darkness and the distant sounds of the city and the warm, wonderful comfort of his arms around her.

4

JUST BEFORE MIDNIGHT, Merry fell asleep. Her sigh caressed Lee's cheek as she relaxed and nestled into the
warming curves of his body. He sighed too, softly, and
shifted to accommodate her.

At one o'clock, he told himself to get some sleep and
to stop thinking about the sensuous feel of her against
him.

A little after two, he scooted to the edge of the bed,
putting some much needed distance between his body
and hers. She followed him, curling around his backside
like a kitten.

By four, his arms ached with the effort it took to keep
from pulling her into a tight embrace. He inched away
from her, intending to get out of bed, settle in the chair
and maybe catch a couple of hours' sleep. But as he
moved to leave, Merry murmured a low protest. Lee
turned on his side and drew her safely into his embrace
again. She stretched against him, her thighs brushing his,
her breasts nudging into the contours of his chest.

He ought to move. He had no business staying in this
compromising position. But her breath warmed the hollows of his throat and her sigh of contentment kept him
still. And he couldn't deny the pleasure he felt just holding her. The situation was impossible, already. But then,
moving away from her wasn't going to do much to rec-
tify it, either.

The soft, even rhythm of her heartbeat thudded against his shoulder and stirred desires he did not want to acknowledge. They were just a man and a woman sharing a bed. Two people. In the darkness.

In the seductive, secretive darkness.

He had to stop thinking about her, about how very womanly she felt in his arms. But how could he think of anything else? He was, after all, a man. He recognized the tense throb in his muscles and the eloquent body language of desire. And he couldn't, wouldn't allow himself anything but the most platonic caress.

Sometime around dawn, he awoke from a dream and pressed a reassuring kiss to the top of her head, but the sleep wouldn't release him and he settled back into its narcotic warmth. The next time he awakened, sunlight spilled through the curtains and the sounds of morning rattled softly in the hallway and purred in the outside world. Merry was still beside him and still asleep. He could tell by the steady rise and fall of her breasts beneath his hand.

Glancing down, he could see that the top buttons of her blouse had come undone and her bra strap had slipped down, exposing the creamy swell of her breast. He moved his fingers lightly to test the texture of her skin. It was soft and silky and the lace of her bra had scored a pattern of pale rosebuds across it.

Reluctantly, he started to adjust the strap and the buttons, but Merry shivered and he stopped. No matter how intimate the setting, he needed to maintain detachment.

"Hmm," she murmured, stirring in his arms. She tipped her head back on the pillow and slowly opened her eyes. A glimpse of mesmerizing blue, screened with sooty dark lashes, met his gaze. Her hair splayed in long, luscious, ebony strands around her face and across her shoulders. Lee raised himself on one elbow to properly appreciate the picture. He'd studied her photographs from every angle, but he'd never seen her look more beautiful than she did at this moment. Either maturity had given her a subtle edge or he had chanced upon a remarkable perspective. There were definite advantages to waking up in the same bed with a woman, he thought. Too bad he had to pretend he was totally unaware of them.

"Hi," he said and smiled.

Another sleepy sound whispered from her throat as Merry brought her arm around Lee's neck and nuzzled into his shoulder. Her mouth pressed against the material of his shirt and a fiery sensation fanned out to the rest of his body. When she lifted her chin, he was waiting and met her lips with as much self-restraint as he could muster.

But temperance didn't come easily. Not with the pressure of her mouth against his, the persuasive femininity of her body nudging his to an excruciating awareness. He didn't want her to know, to feel, how aroused he was. He had to keep control of this embrace, force himself not to notice how good she felt in his arms, how sweet was the taste of her lips.

A moment into the kiss, Merry came fully awake. This was not, she realized, her bed at home. She was not hugging her pillow. And the lips pressed so warmly and possessively against hers did not belong to a shadowy dream lover. He was real. Very real. She drew back, alarmed at the tender feelings whirling through her drowsy thoughts. She looked squarely into dark eyes filled with concern and...desire? No. Not that. Concern, yes, but not...

"Good morning," she said and forced down a sudden sense of alarm. Rolling to the far side of the bed, she slowly swung her feet to the floor. Her blouse gaped open and she buttoned it with one hand, keeping her back to him and shielding her self-conscious movements from his sight. "Did you sleep well?"

"I dropped off almost the minute my head hit the pillow."

Merry pushed the hair away from her temples as she glanced over her shoulder. Lee was stretched out on his side, one large hand supporting a narrow and most attractive jaw. He was long, lean and looked as lazily seductive as any man she'd ever seen. "I thought you were awake long after I'd drifted off."

His mouth curved in a slow smile. "I might have been a little restless. Sorry if I disturbed you."

"No. You didn't. I hope I..." The words trailed into an awkward silence. She felt so strange. For a moment, she could only look into his eyes, seeking whatever shared emotions had bonded them, wondering why everything seemed so different in the morning light. The attraction was still there... she felt its titillating glow deep within her and she wondered why it hadn't vanished with the dawn.

Lee broke the contact and the quiet by getting to his feet and reaching for his shoes. "I guess I took more than my share of the covers. Probably more than Willie would have."

"Probably, but you were warmer. That ought to count for something."

"Good circulation. Are you hungry?"

"No, are you?" Merry began to relax. Nothing had happened. Lee had slept beside her. That was all. The feeling of awkwardness faded into last night's familiarity. "I'm not big on breakfasts."

He shook his head as he smoothed down his clothing and tucked his shirt tail inside his trousers. "Big mistake. You know what they say."

"It's the most important meal of the day. Yes, I've heard."

"Good, then today you can make an exception and join me for breakfast."

"I joined you for dinner last night." And other things as well, but she thought better of mentioning those. "We don't want to start a habit."

"Sure we do. Dinner, breakfast, lunch, midnight snack. All important. All more enjoyable when shared." He paused and his mouth curved in a short smile. "We don't have to enjoy them in any particular order, either. I'm versatile."

Yes, Merry thought, he probably was. "You sound like Molly. Her favorite day at preschool is Backward Day. Everyone walks backward, eats dessert first, wears their clothes inside out and backwards. She loves it."

"I don't blame her. It sounds like fun to me." Lee tried for a nonchalant tone. He didn't want Merry to dwell on the rumpled bed and the fact that she'd just spent the night wrapped around him. He was dwelling on it enough for both of them. "I think I'll go back to my room for a shower—" a cold one, he thought "—and fresh clothes." He glanced down, then brought a laughing gaze to hers. "These look like I slept in them. I might be better off to say it's Backward Day and wear them wrong side out. What do you think?"

Merry shook her head, looking charmingly disheveled and quietly uncertain. "I think I'll shower and change, too. Maybe it'll wash away this anxiety I have about getting on that plane this morning."

Lee wanted to comfort her, draw her into his arms and hold her. Instead, he headed for the door. "You're just hungry. Meet me downstairs in the restaurant in thirty minutes. I'll buy your breakfast."

"That's not neces—"

"No," he interrupted. "But it will give me pleasure." With a hand on the opened door, he offered her a smile and no chance to protest. "See you."

Merry followed him to the door, but he was already gone and she thoughtfully slipped on the safety chain. Lee, she thought. Lee Zurbaron. He had shared her bed and her dreams. And she'd not only slept *beside* him, she'd nestled into his arms like a child burrowing under a mountain of covers on a winter night. She couldn't believe she'd done that. It was out of character for her, so . . . human. With a frown, Merry walked into the adjoining bathroom and studied her face in the mirror.

"So?" she asked her reflection. "You spent the night with a man, a stranger. Nothing happened. What are you worrying about?"

There were a dozen answers, but none of them fit. She hadn't slept with many men. Ian, of course, but before him and after, despite a wealth of offers, she'd avoided intimate situations whenever possible. In her past, she'd known too many men—boys, actually—who'd liked the glamour of her life-style, the way her name conferred status, more than they liked being with her. She'd considered the publicity dating game empty and foolish and she'd never felt—not once—that a boy liked her for who she really was. In truth, she hadn't believed anyone would. Not then.

Lee liked her. He told her in long, appreciative, scintillating glances, in slow, seductive smiles, in exquisite kisses. And right or wrong, she'd surrendered to her own needs last night. She had needed him . . . as a friend, as a buffer against the night, as a man who awakened emotions she hadn't realized she possessed. Was it just the circumstances that made him seem so special . . . a hero? Would she look back at this in a few days and wonder why she'd behaved so recklessly? Or would she remember the experience with tender longing? Would she wish she had done more than sleep beside him?

She'd kissed him last night. And this morning. The memory ran through her like warm honey and abruptly she turned to the shower. In a minute, maybe less, she stood beneath the spray, soaking in the wet heat and trying to ignore the low ache in her stomach. She'd kissed Lee because in that hazy pre-awakening, she'd dreamed of a lover and of his steamy caresses.

Merry ended the shower quickly, trying to deny her desire. She couldn't afford to spend her time and energy on fantasies. Perhaps later, when she'd gained a better perspective on Lee and her feelings about him, she would understand why he evoked such sensual thoughts. But for now, she had very little objectivity.

Besides she had other things to do. In a little less than three hours, she'd be boarding another plane and flying to Houston. Her nerves quivered with the idea, but she ignored their protest. She had to get ready, repack her bag. This was no time to dwell on the night just past. She had a date for breakfast.

"THE CAPTAIN HAS NOW turned off the seatbelt light. . . ."

Merry found she could breathe again. Beside her, Lee squeezed her hand and released it.

"So far, so good," he said. "I didn't bruise your fingers, did I?"

It had been she who had held his hand in a stranglegrip as the plane took off from the Amarillo Airport, but she was glad he didn't say so. She shook her head. "My fingers are fine. Now, if only the plane will land in Houston without scraping its belly on the runway."

"Our arrival in Houston will be uneventful." Lee released his seat from its upright position and shifted back a half-inch. "The odds against another emergency are in our favor."

"What a comfort." Merry frowned and turned to look out the window.

"Are you that worried?"

"I suppose I'm just anxious because of Molly. Yesterday all I could think of was what her life would be like without me in it."

"Well, today, you can think about meeting her in Galveston. That will be much more pleasant."

Merry didn't answer, her thoughts taken up with Molly. It was several minutes before Lee spoke again and his words came slowly, as if he'd meditated on them for a while. "This is my first vacation in three years. I've never been to Texas before. Never visited Houston . . . or Galveston, for that matter." He turned his head and looked at Merry. "Which is a better spot for tourists?"

"That depends on what kind of tourist you plan to be."

"Oh, the usual kind. Bermuda shorts, souvenir T-shirt, camera slung around my neck, traveler's checks in my pockets. You know the type."

Merry smiled at the image. "Most visitors enjoy seeing the Johnson Space Center outside of Houston. Then there's the Astrodome and any number of cultural exhibits. Plenty of fine restaurants, too."

Lee nodded as if considering the attractions. "What does Galveston have to offer?"

"Twenty-five miles of beach and shops."

"That's it?"

"Well, there's the wharf, the Strand, the historical district, Seawolf Park, and all kinds of restaurants and hotels. But mostly, it's beach and shops."

"Would I like it?"

"I don't know." Merry turned toward the window, again. His subtle hints about Galveston lightened her mood. He wanted to be asked to join her on the island. Her heart skipped a beat at the thought and she wondered if she should invite him along. It wasn't such a farfetched idea. And it had definite appeal. "Didn't you tell me you live on the beach in California?"

"I've been staying at my parents' place. House-sitting for them while they travel around like certified retirees. I had a place near the ocean before, but theirs is closer. I can walk out the door and be on the beach in five minutes. It's fairly quiet, too, and I needed a quiet place to work." He paused as if he were waiting for her to question him further. When she didn't, he continued. "I prefer the Pacific to the Atlantic, but I've never seen the Gulf of Mexico, so I don't know how I'd feel about it."

She caught back a smile. "You should make a point of seeing it then, while you're in Houston."

"And you say Galveston has twenty-five miles of beaches? That must be impressive."

"I like it. At least, I did the last time I was there. That was several years ago."

Lee shifted, frowned, and Merry decided to take pity on him. "Why don't you visit Galveston while you're here? It's only an hour's drive from Houston."

"Maybe we could drive over together?"

There, he was all but asking to accompany her. So why was she hesitating? Why not just suggest he join her for the rest of the day? And night. Merry recognized the reasons for her apprehension. Could she spend the day with him and not spend the night? Was this another instance of recklessly following blind impulse into a situation she might later regret? Or would the regret come if she didn't take this one, innocent risk? Lee seemed so nice, so . . . right. What was she afraid of? "I planned to rent a car at the airport," she said.

"I'll take care of that." He leaned toward her, eagerness etched into his expression.

Despite a niggling doubt, Merry gave in with a nod. "Are you sure, Lee? I mean, Galveston's main attraction is the beach and if you live on the Pacific . . ."

"There's more to life and vacations than sand and surf, Merry. I want to spend more time with you. Where we are is not important."

What could she say to that? How could she deny the sliver of excitement that pierced her? How could anyone let caution interfere with this sense of exciting possibilities? She was flattered by his honesty and swayed by the memory of lying in his arms only a few hours ago. This seemed to be her time for acting on impulse. It was amazing what a brush with disaster did for one's outlook. "I'd like that, Lee. I'd really like that."

He settled back and closed his eyes, as if her consent had been a hard-won battle. In truth, he'd won easily because she wanted him with her. She felt strange just admitting that to herself, but it was true. She was, after all, a grown woman and her needs and wants came out in full force with Lee. Not that she believed any long-term relationship would develop between them, but she liked him. She liked him a lot.

Molly would like him, too, Merry thought, and then decided that was irrelevant. She wasn't sure she wanted the two of them to meet. It was one thing for Merry to enjoy the attentions of a man and quite another thing to introduce that man to Molly.

Lee's arm brushed against hers and a scintillating warmth rippled through her. Merry's thoughts jumped back to him and she wondered why her mind was throwing up so many barriers against the attraction awakening within her. Lee posed no threat to her daughter, or to her. He wasn't going to disrupt her life. In fact, after today, he'd probably go on with his vacation and she'd go on with hers and their paths wouldn't cross again. This was just a chance encounter. Something her friends were always telling her she needed. So why shouldn't she enjoy the moment?

If Ian were alive, he'd be saying the same thing. He'd wanted her to be less cautious, more open to the possibility of love. Of course, that had been easy for him to say. Ian had never met a stranger, had never hesitated to trust his instincts or other people. She'd admired that quality in him, even though she recognized her inability to duplicate it. There had been moments during their three-year marriage when she'd wondered if she really trusted him. He had been kind, loving, everything good, and yet she'd never trembled at his touch . . . as she'd trembled last night and this morning in Lee's arms. The memory returned, heated, uncomfortable, and enticing. Impulsively, she reached for his hand, but stopped mid-movement. No, she thought. She no longer needed anyone to hold her hand.

Lee noticed her action and wondered what she was thinking. That it concerned him, he had little doubt. But he could only guess as to how the thoughts made her feel.

For his part, he was shouldering a large chunk of guilt. He'd gotten his way, contrived to be invited along on her trip to Galveston, even won her general acceptance. Emerry Edwards was in the palm of his hand, in a manner of speaking. Unfortunately, she was getting entangled in his feelings for Merry McLennan.

As a psychologist, he was fascinated by Emerry. He knew the questions he wanted to ask, the answers he wanted to analyze. He wanted to know what had happened to her, why she had run away, and how she had grown up to become Merry. But with Merry, he couldn't seem to manage any kind of professional distance. He reacted to her as a man . . . a man attracted to a flesh and blood woman. He wanted to touch her, kiss her, be the friend—and the lover—she needed and perhaps dreamed of.

And that put him in one hell of a position, he decided. For all his understanding of human behavior, he couldn't begin to explain his own. He had looked for Emerry for so long. He couldn't allow a strong physical attraction to jeopardize his research paper. This dissertation was too important to let a romantic interest interfere with his objectivity. He'd worked too hard, come too far.

And all of that meant nothing to him when he looked into Merry's blue eyes.

Lee took his glasses from his pocket and put them on. Picking up an in-flight magazine, he began leafing through the pages. Not that he actually read, but it gave him something to do besides thinking about Merry's hand sitting idly in her lap. Holding her hand had gotten him into this awkward situation in the first place. He'd just have to keep reminding himself that Merry was Emerry and Emerry was a part of his research study. He would have to keep his perspective and keep his hands away from her. He was already acutely aware of the dangers inherent in touching her . . . or kissing her.

Lee hoped he really had as much self-discipline as he'd always prided himself in having, because there was no doubt that being with Merry was going to test his willpower to the limit.

5

GALVESTON ISLAND basked in the golden glow of a late summer afternoon. The surf broke first on the rocks of the jetty, then surged in white-capped waves onto the sand. Sea gulls wheeled and dipped on the air currents over the seawall. Shop doors were closed against the eighty-degree heat and humidity, but opened with a welcoming jingle as tourists entered to hunt for the perfect souvenir. Restaurants advertised their bill of fare on marquees, offering specials from seafood to fast-food. The traffic along Seawall Boulevard traveled at a good clip, but stopped frequently to permit jaywalkers to cross the street and make their way down to the beach.

The atmosphere was carefree, as if everyone knew and accepted that this was a resort town, dedicated to rest and relaxation and therefore, not subject to the mundane problems of other places. The ocean lent a touch of wildness, of freedom and frivolity. Lee fell in love with the town almost before he'd seen a quarter of it and couldn't wait to "get out amongst 'em", as he told Merry.

"It was lucky the hotel had a room for you," Merry said as they walked through the old and opulent lobby toward the front entrance and the seawall beyond. "It's sometimes impossible to get a room here at this time of year. The Hotel Galvez is one of the oldest and most popular places to stay."

"I can see why." Lee pushed open the heavy glass doors and waited for Merry to precede him into the steamy air of the indoor swimming area. They went through another glass-paneled doorway and were outside, passing the outdoor pool and parking lot. Lee glanced over his shoulder at the six-story hotel. "I feel very fortunate that I was able to get an ocean view. Must have been a recent cancellation." He glossed over the explanation, thinking he was more fortunate that Merry hadn't noticed the clerk retrieving his name from the confirmed reservation file. He'd stalled for time, looking around the red and gold lobby while Merry completed her registration form and only when she'd stepped away from the desk had he stepped forward to take care of his own arrangements. He wasn't, he'd decided, cut out for this kind of dishonest behavior.

But now, out in the brisk ocean air, his sin of omission seemed a minor one. Merry smiled as the breeze lifted her hair and tossed it around her face. Laughing, she caught it back and secured it with a bright red scarf. "What shall we do first?" She raised her voice over the roar of the surf.

"I don't know about you, but I want a souvenir. Something overpriced, brightly-colored, and practically useless. A T-shirt ought to do it."

"You're determined to be the quintessential tourist, aren't you?"

His eyes met hers for the space of a heartbeat. He should tell her now that he wasn't a tourist at all. But her expression was light, lively...and lovely. He hadn't seen her like this before and he forgot everything except how enchanting she looked. "I have the camera, the Bermuda shorts, and the sunglasses. All I need now is the T-shirt. Admit it, Merry. You want one, too."

"I don't wear them very often."

"We'll get one you can sleep in, then. How often do you get a chance to buy something like—" he squinted against the sunlight and looked at the merchandise prominently displayed in the nearest shop window "—that?"

Merry followed his gaze to the window and the garish fuchsia-colored cotton T-shirt with a green and fluorescent orange surf monster emblazoned across the front. "I don't think I could sleep while wearing that. But if you like it . . ."

"I like it. If you were wearing that, there'd be no danger of losing you in the crowd."

"What do you mean, in the crowd? In that shirt, I'd stand out anywhere on the planet."

Lee grinned. "Perfect."

In a matter of minutes, he had pulled her inside the shop and insisted that she select a shirt of her choice. He passed over the surf monster in favor of a more modest, but still brightly colored souvenir T-shirt for himself and when Merry protested at his paying for her sleep shirt and the one she'd picked out for Molly, he deferred to her wish.

"I love this place," Lee said when they stepped outside, again. "I'm glad you persuaded me to bypass Houston."

"I did twist your arm, didn't I?"

"Yes, but I forgive you. If I lived in Texas, I'd be vacationing here every month or so."

"If you lived in Texas, Galveston Island wouldn't be that big of an attraction."

"Oh, yes it would. The ocean fascinates me. People who visit the ocean fascinate me. I'd be here a lot."

"Well, it's about a six hour drive from Austin. Ian and I came here once several years ago, but I haven't been back since."

"Painful memories?"

"No, it's not that. I just don't have much time for vacations."

Lee lifted his camera and snapped a picture of a Victorian style house, painted in contrasting shades of purple. "Why not?" he asked. "Does your career take up too much of your time?" He aimed the camera at her and clicked the shutter.

Merry froze. "Don't do that," she said and moved away from him.

"What?" Lee followed, his voice concerned, but piqued with interest. "Take your picture?"

"It makes me self-conscious. Please don't."

"I only want a few photographs as mementos."

"You have a T-shirt." Merry turned and began walking past a slower-moving group of vacationers. How could she explain to him that cameras and photographs were painful memories? She couldn't, not without revealing more of herself to him than she intended.

Lee caught up to her and changed the subject, for which she was grateful. "Do you have to work weekends and holidays at the clinic?"

"Not often, but sometimes it's necessary. Weekends and holidays don't have a lot of meaning for some of my patients, so I can hardly insist on not working when they desperately need and want me."

"But what about Molly?"

"She's always well taken care of, although she'd prefer to have me with her around the clock." Merry glanced toward the ocean, feeling that peculiar aloneness she experienced whenever Molly wasn't with her. "I'm anxious to see her. I've missed her a lot."

"I'll bet she's eager to see you, too. When will they be here?"

"Knowing Janie and Ken, it'll be late afternoon or early evening before they arrive."

"I'm looking forward to meeting your daughter."

Merry's stomach gave a little jump. Did she want Lee and Molly to meet? She'd have to decide one way or the other before tomorrow. At the moment, she didn't know how she felt about it. Or how she felt about much of anything, for that matter. She was enjoying Lee's company, the interest and attention he offered so unassumingly. There'd be time enough for decisions later. For now, well, there was still a lot of Galveston to see.

"Let's take these souvenirs to the hotel," she suggested. "I think you should pay a visit to the Strand. Besides the historical sites there, the shops will make you or break you as a tourist."

"Ah, a challenge. I probably should change into my T-shirt, though, before we go, don't you think?"

"Yes, definitely. I wouldn't want to lose you in the crowd . . . and it *will* be crowded."

"There's no danger. I don't intend to leave your side. There's too much I need to know about you, Merry."

A funny feeling quivered through her as he looked into her eyes. For a second, a silly, wistful second, she hoped he might kiss her. She wanted to experience, again, the sensations she'd felt yesterday in his arms. Old, but familiar yearnings stirred low in her stomach. She couldn't believe she was reacting to Lee this way. For years now, she'd been so careful about the people she trusted, about the friendships she made. And suddenly, with Lee, she tossed caution aside and longed for things a woman should share only with the man she loves. It was not like her, Merry thought. Not like her at all.

During the next few hours, though, from late afternoon to early evening, from sunlight to dusk, Merry caught glimpses of herself in shop windows and noticed how happy and relaxed she looked. There was no escaping the fact that Lee was responsible. He made her laugh, prompted her into saying things she hadn't meant to say, revealing pieces of her life she hadn't meant for him to know about. He asked questions in such a way that she was halfway through the answer before she realized it. It was unsettling, but oddly liberating to tell him openly about her work in physical therapy and the everyday problems of being a single parent. She hardly even hesitated when he turned the conversation to her marriage and Ian.

"I knew Ian for several years before we married," she told Lee. "He was a steady person, very calm and self-assured. We were happy and he was ecstatic when Molly was born. Unfortunately, he lived only a short while after that." Merry paused, remembering that painful time. "It was a difficult period for me."

"Yes," Lee said, affirming her pain and her survival. "You said your husband was older than you?"

"Twenty-seven years." Her lips curved in a sad smile. "I suppose a therapist would say I needed a father figure."

"And did you?"

Merry was quiet for several minutes, walking along the covered sidewalk of the Strand, glancing from time to time in the shop windows. "Maybe I did. I never knew my own father. He wasn't a part of my life. It was only my mother and me and my. . . ."

The words trailed away, but Lee knew what she'd omitted. *Career.* Her childhood had consisted of her mother and modeling. He was willing to bet there'd been little else. Until Ian. A twinge of jealousy threaded through his heart. He could explain her attraction to Ian without knowing more about it. It wasn't unusual for a young girl to choose an older man to fill a vacuum in her life. He realized he was envious of the happiness Merry had known with another man. Regardless of what psychological factors had been at work in the relationship. Regardless of the fact that he, Lee, shouldn't have any feelings about Ian McLennan, one way or another.

Objectivity was becoming more and more illusive with every minute he spent in Merry's company. She captivated him and, against the background of this old and colorful town, he found himself studying her movements, her way of talking, the precise, graceful motions of her body. The information he'd gleaned during the afternoon wouldn't fill a dissertation, but he examined every piece of it as if it were a string of priceless pearls.

Merry fascinated him, intrigued him...disturbed him. She brought out a primal need to protect and possess her. Feelings he'd never known before. The bond between them had been forged in a moment, but it held with the strength of a long-standing commitment. He hadn't expected that. He hadn't expected to feel this way at all.

Knowing her background, he'd assumed her personality would be flawed in one way or another. But the more he learned, the more he wondered how a child who'd received the kind of adulation she'd received could have matured into a woman who seemed so unselfish, so considerate of others. Her commitment to her work was admirable, her attitude toward life was unassuming and not nearly demanding enough to his way of thinking. Merry was a "giver" and, by all accounts, she should have been just the opposite.

Lee wondered if he was really getting a clear picture. There were hidden depths to Merry and he was looking at her through rose-tinted glasses. Not to mention the unprofessional and intense longings he experienced every time he thought about holding her in his arms, awakening to her kiss. He couldn't escape those titillating fantasies, no matter what logic he used. Even now, in the midst of a crowded sidewalk, he wanted to catch her against him and capture her lips with his own.

He wouldn't, though. He was, at least, still able to exercise that much control.

"Tell me about being a physical therapist, Merry," he said as they drove back to the Hotel Galvez. "How many patients do you work with at one time? And are they young, old, or in-between?"

"We get all sizes, shapes and temperaments at the Burnstein Clinic. My caseload varies, but I see ten to twelve patients a day. Sometimes I might have two in therapy together. Every case is different." Merry rummaged in one of the sacks and pulled out a pair of sunglasses. With a little smile of satisfaction, she put on the glasses and settled them on the bridge of her nose. "There," she said, her tone brimming with pleasure. "Do these look as good in the car as they did in the store? The lens seems kind of dark."

"That could be because it's dusk." Lee glanced at her to appraise the glasses, but knew he wasn't going to tell her the truth. He liked seeing her eyes and the myriad of expressions that caused the deep blue color to lighten or darken with her mood. The sunglasses were fine—he just didn't like the barrier they created. "They look great. Aren't you glad I talked you into buying them?"

"You're a bad influence, Lee. I'll be paying for this trip for the next year and a half."

Merry hadn't allowed him to pay for anything. Not even the float they'd shared in the Ice Cream Parlor. He wasn't really bothered by her insistence that they go "dutch," but he recognized her efforts to keep him at a distance.

Leaning forward, Lee checked street signs, making sure they were returning the way they'd come. "With all the things you bought today, it's a good thing you have a steady job. Speaking of which, you were telling me about your caseload."

"There's not much to tell." Merry shrugged a dainty, slightly sunburned shoulder. "Besides, you haven't said a word about your work."

Because she hadn't asked before now. Lee felt suddenly like he had passed a difficult test with flying colors. Now, perhaps, he could work his way around to telling her about his dissertation. "I'm a psychologist. I'm working on my... doctorate." He gave a short laugh. "Sometimes I think I've been working on it all my life. But it'll all be over soon." The last sentence left an odd taste in his mouth. He couldn't seem to find the right words. The words that would tell her why he'd had to meet her.

"So what do you do for a living, while you're working toward the degree?"

"I counsel troubled children and their families. At least, I used to. I resigned a few months ago so I could work full time on my doctorate. My parents needed someone to stay at their house, I had a cash offer for my condo, and I grabbed the opportunity. Everything just worked out. So here I am."

"Taking a vacation."

Lee felt trapped and decided now was as good a time as any. "Yes, well, it's more like a working vacation. I brought my research with me and came looking for..." He hesitated one second too long.

"Inspiration in the Gulf of Mexico?" Merry filled in for him. "I've heard people say it's easier to write a dissertation away from home, away from familiar routines and well-meaning family and friends. But I don't know. You'll have to let me know how it works out." She squinted, smoothed the lines on her forehead with a fingertip, and pulled off the sunglasses. "You're right, Lee. It's getting too dark for these." She tucked the glasses inside her purse. "It must be awfully difficult to counsel young children and adolescents," Merry said. "I could never do that."

Lee couldn't decide if he was frustrated or relieved that the opportunity had slipped past. "Don't you work with kids in physical therapy? I thought you said you worked with all ages."

"I do. But working with a child's body is far easier than working with his mind. I don't think I could handle the emotional stress."

It was the closest she'd come to mentioning her own childhood and the resulting anxiety. Lee started to push for more information, but as the Hotel Galvez loomed before them, a white giant against a twilight sky, he let the moment and her comment pass. "Here we are, ma'am," he said as he drove into the covered drive at the rear entrance. "We'll get one of the stewards to help you with all these priceless mementos and I'll park the car. Just take everything to your room and we'll sort it out later."

Merry turned toward him in the car. "Thank you, Lee. It's been a lovely day and I—"

He touched her cheek and the heat radiated through his fingers to the inner parts of his body. "It's not over, Merry. I'll pick you up at your room in an hour. We'll have dinner and then, maybe, we'll check out the lounge." He pressed a fingertip against her lips and felt a powerful longing to place his mouth there, moist and demanding. He swallowed. "Take care of . . . my souvenirs."

Merry's tongue touched her lips and her eyes held his for a long, breathless moment. Then she nodded, smiled and opened the car door. A doorman stepped forward to assist her with the packages. Lee watched her walk up the steps and into the hotel before he drove through the portico to the parking area beyond.

Merry climbed the stairs, a strange excitement swirling around her. Lee had touched her. She'd thought for a moment he was going to kiss her. Silly. They'd been parked in a public place with a doorman watching their every move. But it wasn't silly, because she knew he'd wanted to kiss her. She knew he had thought about the taste of her lips, even as she had thought about the taste of his.

Merry tapped her foot as she waited for the elevator. She smiled at the porter, concealing her distraction behind a well-rehearsed facade. No one would guess she was aquiver with awakening emotions and a vague anticipation. She'd learned early in life to display a cool edge of composure, allowing no one to see past the outer image to her inner self. No one except Lee. And she hadn't actually *allowed* him inside; he'd just somehow found his own way.

She moved into the open elevator and watched the attractive young doorman follow with the shopping bags. She pushed the button for her floor and cautioned herself not to give this vacation romance too much importance. It wasn't really even a romance.

But it had *possibilities*, as Janie would say. Merry couldn't believe she was dwelling on it. Tonight she'd have dinner with Lee and tomorrow...

Tomorrow it would be over.

The elevator arrived at the sixth floor and Merry took out her room key. After tipping the porter, she looked through the sacks and separated her purchases from Lee's, setting his souvenirs aside to give to him later. Then, with a glance at her watch, she sorted through the clothes in her suitcase. She hadn't packed anything suitable for a dinner date, except— Merry pulled out a soft, blue dress of rayon challis and eyed it critically. She moved to the bathroom and held up the dress for inspection in the mirror.

The color was right, the lines feminine and cool, the silhouette clingy. If she hung it in the bathroom while she showered, the steam would melt out any wrinkles and leave the dress smooth and ready to wear. She flipped the skirt, holding it out to one side. It would do, she decided.

Merry studied her reflection for a moment, remembering a time in her life when she'd worn beautiful, expensive clothes and had thought nothing of it. There had always been someone there to steam out any wrinkles, make sure every accessory was available, take care of details like shoes and hosiery and undergarments. How Emee had loved the glamour of it. How she, Merry, had grown to hate it.

Merry whisked the dress on a hanger and hooked it over the door. Then she turned on the shower and gathered her toilet articles. As she stepped naked under the spray, she thought of Lee once again. She cupped her breasts in her hands and stroked their fullness, massaged the tight ache in her nipples. What was wrong with her? She'd never felt so lonely, so . . . needy. And Lee had given no indication that he . . .

But he had. She was only fooling herself if she pretended not to recognize the layers of tension between them. Her breath bunched in her throat each time he looked at her. Even now, alone with the thought of him, her heart pounded a message of intimate yearnings. Yearnings, desires she hadn't experienced before. But she recognized them.

Oh, yes, she recognized them.

She soaped her breasts, the flat planes of her stomach, the long length of her thighs, and imagined how it would feel if Lee were touching her there . . . and there. What would she be doing if he were in the shower with her? His nude body wet and sultry beneath the onslaught of the spray and her searching hands?

Abruptly, Merry shut off the water and pushed shaky hands through the long, drenched tendrils of her hair. This was madness, she thought. A fine, seductive madness. She wondered if she could get through the night without succumbing to its siren call.

"MORE WINE?"

Merry frowned at her almost empty goblet, knowing she shouldn't. "Maybe a little."

Lee poured the Chablis—a little in her glass, a little in his. "Here's to Galveston." He lifted his drink in a toast and raised the glass to his lips.

"And to a room full of worthless souvenirs." She took a sip, but her eyes and her thoughts were on him, on the way his mouth curved against the crystal, the way he held the glass. His hands were large, capable of crushing the wine goblet, but instead he cradled it with delicate strength. The image evoked a ripple of response, a provocative thread of memory. The wine in her glass swirled in reaction to the sudden tension in her hand.

"Once you're home, you can take those almost worthless souvenirs to the clinic and give them to your patients. The gifts will be appreciated and you'll still have had the pleasure of doing the shopping."

"And the pleasure of paying for it."

Lee set down his glass. "Are you worried about the money? Because if you are, I'd be more than happy to—"

"No." Merry interrupted his near-offer of financial assistance. "I'm not worried about money. I have this tendency to believe there's never enough, that a soup line is on the horizon. It's one of those hold over concerns from childhood, I guess. My mother's legacy to her daughter."

"That's surprising. I would have thought . . ."

Whatever Lee had thought, it ended there. He didn't finish the sentence and Merry toyed with the idea of telling him how she'd struggled to detach herself from Emee's idea that money could be equated with happiness. "I didn't grow up in poverty, if that's what you're thinking. In fact, I had everything a child could possibly dream of having."

Lee leaned forward, his eyes dark and probing. "Material things, you mean. There is such a thing as poverty of spirit, Merry."

A wave of distress sluiced through her, as it always did when she spoke of the past. With a shrug of her shoulder, she dismissed the subject and reestablished her mask of composure. "Are you going to have dessert?" she asked.

Lee continued to gaze at her. "That's it, isn't it? This afternoon, when you said it was easier to work with a child's body than with his mind, it was because of *your* childhood, your own experience."

She felt a painful throbbing at the back of her throat. "No, not at all. There are givens in physical therapy, proven techniques that strengthen weak muscles, restore the normal functions of the joints. There aren't those absolutes in psychology. You must know that."

"I know there's no certainty in any therapy, physical or emotional. You're fooling yourself if you think you're not working with your patients' minds as well as with their bodies."

Merry had long ago learned how to derail a potential invasion of her privacy, and she sensed that she should do so now. Even though, deep in some inner corner of her heart, she longed to pour out her story to Lee. "You're right," she said, her lighter tone belying the tension she felt. "Humans are nothing if not complex. Take me, for example. Right now, all I can think about is taking off my shoes and wading in the ocean. Now, how did my mind jump from dinner to psychology to a walk in the Gulf? Complex, right?"

"Not at all. Let's hit the beach." Lee placed his napkin on the table with a smile that was somewhat less than sincere. He knew what she was doing, knew she wanted him to forget what she'd said about her childhood. Why didn't he tell her now that he knew all about Emerry? Why not open his mouth and explain how he knew? That would put an end to this mental game of hide-and-seek.

It might also put an end to everything else and Lee couldn't take that chance. Not yet, anyway.

He followed her from the restaurant and the hotel with a wavering sense of justification. There was no excuse for continuing this charade. He'd told himself he needed time to know her as she was now, in order to better understand how the past had changed her. He'd had last night, all day today. How much more time could he legitimately claim in the interest of research?

Lee knew the answer. None. He was pushing the limits of professionalism. He had to tell her who he was and why he was interested in her. And yet, as he took her hand and walked with her across the street to the seawall, he knew that whatever he told her now would be partly a lie. He was interested in Emerry, yes, but he was also intrigued by Merry.

"Isn't it gorgeous?" Merry's voice filled with soft wonder. "There's something so breathtaking about the ocean. It must be the constancy of the waves, the steadiness of the sound. Like a heartbeat."

Lee could hardly hear anything for the pulsing beat of his own heart. "The full moon doesn't hurt, either," he said and tried not to think about the romantic atmosphere of the moonlight and the ocean and the nearly deserted beach. He held Merry's elbow, supporting her as she slipped off her shoes, then he led the way down the steps to the sand below. "Be careful," he advised. "There are sharp rocks."

"And shells. Tomorrow Molly will hunt seashells until we're both sunburned and tired and have a whole bucketful to take home with us."

"I may do the same. Do you think the shells from the Gulf will be any different from the ones in the Pacific?"

"I doubt it. But be my guest." She gestured toward the beach. "But don't expect me to carry your shells back to the hotel in my shoes. They wouldn't hold much."

He smiled at her teasing tone, liking the almost flirty toss of her head, the sparkle in her eyes. Desire whispered to his senses when she stepped from the rocky seawall to the grainy sand and her mouth parted in a little cry of pleasure. He knew the setting was dangerous. If he had any sense, he'd suggest they retire early—to their separate rooms—and meet again in the bright light of day.

But there was too much moonlight to allow any degree of perspective and as they walked, the voices of reason fell further and further behind. He wanted to kiss her and knew he would before their walk was over.

Merry's hand found its way into his, threading fingers and a warm loop of sensuous feelings through his body. For a while they talked about nothing in particular, but gradually the lulls in conversation lengthened and the silence grew long, broken only occasionally by one or the other of them. When she stopped and stared for long moments at the horizon, he did the same, aware of the growing tension between them . . . and of the inevitable result.

When she finally turned toward him, it was as if he'd been waiting for this all of his life and his arms enclosed her without hesitation. He was at once gentle and rough in his possession, taking from her the sweet taste of a yearning as strong as his, a desire that matched his in intensity. She didn't pull away from the kiss as she'd done that morning. Instead, her hands splayed at his back, moving in sensuous circles, giving pleasure everywhere she touched.

Lee couldn't help himself. He knew better than to get involved in a passionate embrace with Merry, but he found himself bewitched by the feel of her lips beneath his, the press of her body against him. He felt the tentative brush of her tongue against his teeth and a slow heat swirled and spiraled within him. With measured movements, he nudged open her lips and found a way inside. She moaned softly at the invasion, then met his probing tongue with her own. His hand moved to the molded shape of her breast and settled there, palm covering nipple, thumb stroking the rounded slope.

With teasing nibbles, he lowered his mouth to her throat and in a series of tiny kisses, traced the contours of her neck and shoulders. Her skin was soft—so very soft—and smelled of warm sand and salty ocean air. Lee was intoxicated with the taste and scent of her. He couldn't remember ever being so lost to the world that he'd forgotten where he was and why he was there and what he'd meant to do.

But it had happened now. She felt so good in his arms, so perfectly formed for his body, so sweetly responsive to his touch. He could only respond to the fiery blaze of emotions inside him. And even as the first flames subsided to a gentler, more reasonable ardor, he continued to bask in the warmth. He savored the moment and the night and the sounds of the waves hitting the sand...and the woman in his arms.

Merry quivered beneath an onslaught of mixed emotions and reckless yearnings. It had been a long time since a man had held her and touched her. She knew she'd never experienced this hungry ache in her body. Not with Ian, not with anyone. Since his death, she'd been kissed only a few times and none had consisted of more than a simple meeting of lips. With Ian, she had shared tender, deeply affectionate kisses . . . but there had been nothing like the passion she felt now. Nothing with the sheer force of desire that rocked her physically and emotionally in the circle of Lee's arms.

She responded without protest, accepting the strong bonding that drew her to him and the powerful chemistry of desire. In her past, she had observed lust, had learned to recognize its reflection in a man's eyes when he looked at her. And she had thought of it as something to shun, something frightening and coarse. But suddenly, experiencing feelings over which she had no control and little mastery, she wondered if lust could be an integral part of a man-woman relationship. She felt it now . . . and she wasn't scared. Not by any stretch of the imagination.

She wanted Lee. Her body pulsed with the need to be closer to him. Her heart throbbed with longings buried deeply for too many years. Was it wrong? She'd only known him a little more than a day.

But it didn't matter. She understood that, at least. When he kissed her, nothing else mattered.

When Lee lifted his mouth from hers, Merry had to exert tremendous effort to keep her lips from clinging to his. She breathed deeply of the salty ocean air and summoned composure from some shadowy corner of her mind. It was one thing for her to realize how lost to propriety she had been and quite another for him to realize she knew. She moistened her lips and turned her gaze to the waves pounding against the rock jetty.

Lee was breathing heavily. But he had to do something, say anything to keep her from realizing how the kiss had affected him. He'd never lost control of himself that way. Never before, anyway.

He stood beside her, very close, and waited for his body to stop clamoring for more. He wanted to make love to her—here—on the beach. Seductive scenes flashed through his mind, tantalizing, intriguing, compelling. But this was a public beach. He respected Merry, and himself, too much to submit to a passion born in moonlight and nurtured by wine and a romantic setting.

"We should never have come out here while the moon was full," he said after his breathing had steadied. "I told you it was dangerous."

"You only told me I should be careful."

"I wish you'd taken my advice."

"And missed the most romantic souvenir of the day?"

"As I recall, you've described all the other souvenirs as worthless."

She smiled. One of those Mona Lisa kind of smiles that said nothing and yet told him everything. Here, on the beach, with the moonlight and the gentle surf, he could almost pretend they were simply a man and a woman on the brink of falling in love.

He'd known her a little more than a day. How could he so completely have lost sight of his objective? "We'd better get back to the hotel," he said. "It's getting late and you have a date with a seashell collector tomorrow, remember?"

"I'll be free in the morning, though." She turned to him and pressed her hand lightly to his cheek. Her blue eyes held his in the darkness. "I believe I owe you a breakfast."

"You're determined to keep this on a dutch treat basis, aren't you?"

She shrugged a dainty shoulder. "These are the nineties, Lee. Be glad I didn't take you up on your offer to pay for my shopping spree this afternoon."

"I would have with the greatest pleasure."

"Well, it will give me pleasure to buy your breakfast in the morning. Is it a date?"

How could he refuse? "It's a date. What time?"

There was a pause that lasted a heartbeat, no longer. "Whatever time we wake up."

Invitation was in her voice. She might be unaware of it, guileless, but he heard it and tried to convince himself he could accept. He wanted her so badly he could almost taste the rich satisfaction making love with her would bring. All he had to do was say the right words and she would sleep in his arms again tonight. He squeezed her hand and prepared to battle the temptation all the way to her door.

They walked silently back to the hotel. The lobby was quiet, summoning in its solitude. The elevator enclosed them with privacy and a pulsing expectancy. Lee had never been more aware of vulnerability...both hers and his own. He felt helpless, confused and absolutely sure that he could not, should not stay with her tonight.

When she unlocked the door to her room and turned to him, he drew a deep breath and cupped her face in his hands. "Thank you, Merry, for one of the loveliest days I've ever spent. You're a beautiful, exciting woman and I...hope you sleep well." He brushed his fingertip across her cheek and down to the corner of her mouth. "Dream of me."

Her lips curved beneath his touch and the desire to kiss her surged through him, testing him, tempting him. The anticipation quickened to a painful longing and Lee tried to reason it away, tried to warn his misguided intentions. He would tell her now. He would open his mouth and explain why he'd wanted to meet her, how he'd managed to find her. And then.... Then if she wanted him to stay...

"Your souvenirs, Lee." Merry stepped back into the shadowy hallway of her room. "I almost forgot to give them to you. They're here. I put everything in one sack." She turned away from him and he heard the rustle of paper. He could feel his resistance crumpling like the paper, folding in upon itself, wrinkling into new patterns he couldn't smooth out.

"Merry, I want to—"

"Lee," she began at the same moment in a voice both soft and supplicating. "Please, I—"

He could hardly breathe and then somehow, she was in his arms, her face lifted to his. He knew he was on dangerous ground. He should have been more careful, more honest. With her and with himself. Now he wondered if he'd waited too late. But her lips were on his, her body entreating and enticing him and he was lost.

Merry was silk—cool and inviting, smooth and alluring. He could not hold her close enough, or find a single place on her skin that did not whisper out for his touch. He followed the contours of her cheek to the shadowed softness of her throat. He stroked the curve of her spine, bunching the fabric of her dress in his hand and imagining the warm, satiny flesh beneath.

Merry wanted to relax in the strong support of Lee's arms. She was torn between a reckless desire to surrender to their mutual passion and the inhibiting voice of caution. This shouldn't be happening. But her palm pressed flat against his racing heartbeat and the quick, throbbing rhythm flowed into her and around her until nothing made sense. Her body was taut with need, and when he found the buttoned closure of her dress and slid the material from her shoulders, she shivered and told herself to protest, to stop this now before it went too far. But the only thing she could force from her throat was a deep and satisfied sigh. It felt good. So very good.

The dress slipped down past her breasts, over her hands, clung momentarily at her waist and then rippled into a soft, muted pool of blue at her feet. She heard Lee's swift intake of breath, felt the tension in his upper arms as he lifted her against him and laid her on the end of the bed.

He was beside her before she had time to miss the warmth of his body. As soon as her lips hungered for him, he was kissing her again. A hot, eager ache of desire flooded her senses and she wondered if this was how it felt to lose all reason, all inhibition. She knew she had to stop him, but dear God, how did she begin?

Lee rained a series of sipping kisses along the slope of her breast, easing aside the lacy edge of her bra. He wanted it to vanish, to leave her exposed to his gaze, his touch. But even as he thought of removing the lacy impediment his hand trembled at her waist. It was too soon. She didn't know enough about him. He had no way of protecting her. And he would not—*would not*—violate her trust.

Moments passed, one slow, agonizing moment after another as he fought for his lost control. Finally he drew a long, steadying breath and moved away from temptation. "Merry, I—" What would he say? How could he excuse his lapse of judgment? "I'm sorry. I shouldn't have allowed that to happen."

Her sigh shimmered with a dozen regrets. "I don't understand, Lee. This is not... I don't lose control like this. I'm not ... easy."

"I know." How well he knew. "I'm not accustomed to losing control, either. There's something so special, so desirable about you, Merry.... But that's no excuse. I'm sorry."

"You don't have to sound so miserable about it, Lee. We're both adults." She rolled onto her side, facing him. "An apology seems sort of ... dishonest."

Her breath was misty-sweet against his face and he felt desire stir and protest again. But he knew that *dishonest* pretty well summed up his feelings at the moment. "Think of it as an apology that I didn't come...prepared to love you tonight. I didn't bring any... protection."

"Oh." Understanding crept eloquently into the single syllable. "I didn't think of that."

"Neither did I." If he had, would he have brought something to guard against the possible consequences? he wondered. Or would he have talked himself out of the idea long before the question even arose? "I think we need to talk, Merry. There are things you need to know about me."

Apprehension skipped through her like a stone upsetting the smooth surface of a lake. "Yes," she said. "But not tonight, Lee. Not here." She didn't want to know, Merry thought. Whatever it was he thought he had to tell her, it could wait. Tomorrow this dream, this strange bond between them, would come to an end. Tomorrow Molly would arrive and with her the reality of motherhood and responsibilities. Tonight Merry wanted to believe in magic. The magic that had almost, *almost* happened between them. She needed time to think, time to understand the effect Lee had on her. Time to regain her precious control. "Tomorrow," she whispered. "We'll talk tomorrow."

A hesitancy hung in the air and Merry moved away from it and from him, discouraging him from encroaching on the silence. She reached for her robe and slipped into it, feeling her composure begin to return slowly. They had been out of control and careening toward disaster. She should be relieved that he'd taken the initiative to end their embrace.

This time when she stood in the hallway with Lee, she was very conscious of maintaining a discreet distance. Lee looked at her, his eyes mysterious and shadowed. If he said a word, whispered her name, she'd be in his arms again. She knew it and wondered at her weakness.

Merry's eyes were on him, confused and troubled in the dim light shining in from the outside hall. Lee checked the impulse to touch her as he said a soft goodnight and left her to sleep alone . . . and perhaps to dream of him. His body ached with the tension, but he knew that, perhaps for the wrong reasons, he had made the right choice.

6

MERRY AWAKENED LATE, but felt refreshed and ready to face Lee. Her skin went hot whenever she thought of last night . . . on the beach, in her room. But she felt in control this morning. The old habits of composure and reserve were reinstated. She was ready to keep this odd, scintillating attraction in perspective. Today was the last day she would be alone with Lee. She'd probably never see him again after this weekend. And with that thought in mind, she went downstairs to meet him for a midmorning breakfast buffet.

Stepping out of the elevator, she saw Lee waiting for her at the entrance to the dining area, and walked toward him. A smile bloomed slowly on his lips. Last night, she thought, those lips had stolen her heart with kisses, taken her hostage and—

"Mommy! Mommy!"

Merry whirled at the call, delight and dismay blending together as she bent and held out her arms to catch a small child with flyaway, dark curls. "Molly, Molly," she said softly as she wrapped the little girl into a big hug. "Oh, I'm so happy to see you. I didn't expect to see you so soon."

Lee watched mother and daughter kiss and squeeze and eventually win the attention of almost every person passing through the great open lobby. They were a striking pair with matching blue eyes and long, silky hair. Molly had the look of her mother, despite a lingering toddler chubbiness, but where Merry's smile was reserved, Molly's was open and welcoming. When she turned her baby charm on him, Lee knew she'd won his heart.

"Hello," Molly said, sounding quite grown-up for a three-year-old.

Merry glanced up with a wistful smile and a sure hold on her child. "This is Lee, Molly. Lee, this is my daughter."

Lee went down to her level, but he wasn't sure if it was because of his training with children or simply because Molly seemed to expect it. "It's nice to meet you, Molly," he said. "Your mother has told me a great deal about you."

Wide blue eyes flew to mother to check the truth of that before returning to Lee with new assessment. "H'lo," she said again and wrapped her arms around Merry's neck. "Can we swim, Mommy? Willie and me want to swim."

"*Willie?* I think it's Molly who wants to swim." Merry gently emphasized the name of her daughter's imaginary friend, thereby acknowledging that Willie was not real, but that it was all right for Molly to pretend. Lee admired Merry all the more for her quiet acceptance of Molly's imagination.

"Please, Mommy, can we?" Molly asked again.

"In a bit, darling." Merry rose, bringing Molly with her. For a moment—one long moment—Merry's eyes met Lee's. He glimpsed regret in their depths and wondered what she was thinking, what she was feeling. Before Molly ran across the lobby, he had been contemplating how to tell her all he'd failed to tell her last night, but now...

"I thought we'd never get here." A petite, blond woman set an overflowing beach bag on the floor beside Merry and sighed wearily after the two little girls who raced around, then past her to the doors leading to the indoor pool. A tall, thin man, with a suitcase under one arm and two overstuffed bags in each hand stopped beside her. "Ken drove like a maniac, but it wasn't fast enough for these girls." The blonde was obviously speaking to Merry, but her gaze was fixed on Lee. "Carol woke us all at four o'clock this morning and by five, all three of them were in the car, honking the horn and yelling that they were ready to 'see the sea'. Of course, they all went to sleep and Ken and I were left to drink coffee and drive like fools."

Molly wiggled and Merry set her free to race after the other girls before making the introduction her friends so obviously anticipated. "Janie, Ken, this is Lee Zurbaron. Lee, my friends, Ken and Janie Lester and, over by the pool doors, their daughters, Carol and Katy."

Lee stepped forward, offering his hand to Ken, who dumped all the suitcases in order to complete the handshake. "It's nice to meet you," Lee said politely.

"We're certainly glad to meet *you*." Janie shifted a meaningful "you've-been-holding-out-on-us" look to Merry. "I'll check in," Janie told Ken. "You keep the girls from breaking something." With that, she walked to the registration desk.

"How are you, Merry?" Ken asked with a keen glance at Lee. "I understand you had an exciting trip down here."

"Exciting is one way to describe it." Merry's eyes flicked to Lee's, and he knew she was remembering the moments that had brought them together. "It sounds like your trip from Austin wasn't uneventful, either. Did you really drive like a 'fool'?"

"You know how Janie exaggerates. Especially after several hours in the car with the kids." He tossed an affectionate look toward his daughters, but his gaze drifted back to Lee with a certain air of appraisal. "Molly wasn't a problem, though. We've enjoyed having her with us while you were gone, Merry. She's been anxious to get here and be with her mama, though."

"I've been anxious to be with her, too. Especially after the incident in Amarillo."

"I'll bet. Must have been pretty frightening." Ken shook his head. "Were you there, too?" he asked Lee.

"Yes." Lee didn't know what else he could add without perjuring himself. He liked Ken. The man seemed friendly, even though he clearly was sizing up Lee as an acceptable acquaintance for Merry. Lee thought he might have a strong ally in Janie Lester, but it was a little early to tell. He sensed that Merry's friends cared about her and wanted her to have the best.

"Look, Daddy." One of the Lester children waved for her father's attention.

Ken turned to nod and wave in an absent, fatherly manner. "Are you from around here?" he asked Lee directly. "Texas? Louisiana?"

"California." Lee slipped a hand in his hip pocket, feeling ill at ease. "Near San Diego."

The two men went through the motions of discovery, much like strange dogs sniffing to determine if the other was friend or foe. Merry decided to rescue Lee. "Lee's never been to the Gulf before," she explained to Ken. "I've been showing him around."

"Oh," Ken said. "Oh, well, that's good. There's a lot to see."

"The only thing I want to see is a bed with clean sheets." Janie rejoined the group, completing the foursome. "Maid service. That's the best reason to stay in a hotel. Someone else picks up. Speaking of which, we have a room and can go up any time we like." She dangled a key in front of Ken's nose. "So, lover boy, got any plans for the afternoon?"

"A nap." A wide grin cut across Ken's lean face. "But I could be yours to command, my amazon. If the price is right . . ."

Janie laughed as she reached down to grab her beach bag. "Isn't he cute?" she said to no one in particular. "All right, let's get this show on the road . . . or more accurately, the beach. Ken, why don't you and Lee take the bags up to our room while Merry and I take the girls to her room and let them change into their swimsuits." She arched a sandy eyebrow in Merry's direction. "Okay, with you? I don't know how long we can keep these darling children happy without taking them to 'see the sea'."

Merry turned to Lee, her eyes alight with happiness, her lips curved with subtle amusement. "Do you mind helping Ken with the bags?"

At that moment, he wouldn't have minded if she'd asked him to polish all the silver in the dining room. "I'd be glad to. Provided, that is, that I'm invited to join you in this family outing."

"Of course." Janie hefted the beach bag onto her shoulder and motioned to the children. "You don't think we'd pass up the opportunity for adult conversation, do you? Ken and I have too many discussions about ponytails and preschools. Sometimes I think we developed a cartoon mentality about the time the girls turned two and three." Janie strode to the elevator with her two blond daughters and Molly in tow.

Merry hung back, sliding her hand into Lee's in quick apology. "I didn't expect them to be here until this evening."

"It's all right. We'd probably have spent the day collecting worthless souvenirs, anyway."

"Yes, but—" She didn't finish the statement and Lee was glad. His heart already was beating too fast for comfort. "Will you go with us to the beach?"

"I was only waiting for you to second the motion."

They exchanged a squeeze of fingers behind the cover of Merry's full skirt, then Merry went to join her friend, leaving Lee with Ken, the suitcases and who knew what further line of questioning.

She was aware that Lee watched her as she walked away and the knowledge settled inside her like the warmth of a lighted window on a cold night. She hadn't known she wanted him to meet her friends—and Molly—until their arrival. Then suddenly she'd known how important it was that they meet.

For an instant, her eyes met Lee's and her breath hung precariously in her throat. He had such a profound effect on her. Was this how it felt to fall head over heels for a guy? After all these years, could it really be so simple?

"Okay," Janie said under her breath. "Who is he?"

Merry ignored Janie's insinuating expression and pretended nonchalance. "Lee? Oh, I met him on the plane."

"The one to Houston or the one that bit the dust in—"

"We met on the Denver flight—" Merry intercepted, glancing warningly at the children. She didn't want to talk about the accident in Molly's presence "—shared . . . dinner . . . in Amarillo, flew on to Houston, and drove to Galveston together."

"He just *happened* to be going to Galveston?"

"I believe he'd originally planned to vacation in Houston, but he changed his mind."

"And we know why, don't we?" Janie's smile was a study in satisfaction. "Well, all I can say is, it's about time."

That wasn't all Janie wanted to say and once they reached the hotel room, it became obvious her curiosity was boundless. Between helping Molly into her swimsuit and trying to defuse Janie's determination to know more about Lee, Merry had her hands full.

"Have you slept with him?" Janie came close to whisper.

Merry glanced at her friend and arched a discouraging brow. "I've only known him a couple of days."

Janie lifted her shoulders in a 'So, what?' shrug. "Well, have you?"

"Katy's strap is twisted." Merry reached for the toddler and refastened the swimsuit before she stood up. "There, are we all ready to go?"

"You should put on your swimsuit, Merry." Carol, the five-year-old, announced with authority. "And Mom doesn't have hers on, either."

"I forgot to bring mine," Janie said in mock regret.

"It's in the bag, Mom," Carol insisted. "I put it in for you."

"Oh, thank you, honey." Janie smiled appreciatively at her daughter before making a sour face behind her back. "So much for keeping this cellulite under wraps," she whispered to Merry.

"Put yours on, Mommy." Molly danced from the ocean view window to the middle of the room and back. "Hurry! The waves are coming!"

Ken tapped on the door. "Any beach bunnies in there?" he called, eliciting squeals of delight from the girls. Janie gathered Carol and Katy, sandals and towels and dumped it all into her husband's arms when she opened the door. "Go on down," she instructed. "Merry and I have to change. We'll meet you at the indoor pool in about—" she looked to Merry for agreement "—ten minutes, okay?"

Merry nodded, encouraging Molly to accompany Ken and his girls to the pool. There were murmurs in the hallway. Merry heard Lee's voice, but couldn't make out the words. Still, just the low timbre, the cadence of his voice warmed her. *Pretend I'm your imaginary friend,* he'd told her that first night. Her lips curved with the memory.

"If I weren't so crazy about Ken," Janie said as she closed the door, "I'd make a play for your beau. He has a fine-looking backside. Did you notice?"

Merry grabbed her swimsuit and headed for the bathroom. "No," she said. "I hadn't."

"Give me a break. You may as well tell me everything now, because I'll wheedle it out of you, Merry. You know I will."

Merry closed the bathroom door. "We met on the plane. He's been very nice. What else do you want to know?"

"Details." Janie's voice was muffled now, but slightly raised to carry from the bedroom to the bath. "Have you slept with him?"

"You're very nosy."

"I am, I admit it. So tell me."

Merry pulled on the turquoise suit and adjusted the straps for comfort. She hardly glanced in the mirror as she began pinning her hair into an upsweep. There was a tap on the door and a plaintive whine. "Merry, this is not fair. You haven't given a man the time of day for years and suddenly you introduce me to this guy...and you're smiling. You look . . . happy. Can you blame me for wanting to know more?"

"There's nothing to know, Janie. I swear." Merry caught the reflection of her smile and stopped to inspect it. Was it true? Was there something different about her? She looked the same. She felt the same.

No, she didn't. She felt . . . renewed.

But she wasn't going to tell Janie. Or anyone else. What she'd shared with Lee was special. And private. She only wished she'd been more open with him sooner. She hadn't asked enough questions, hadn't found out nearly enough about him. And yet, she didn't think there was anything that would change her mind. Lee was not like the men in her past, not like the people who'd wanted to use her. He didn't even know about her past. And last night, when he could have made love to her with abandon, he'd chosen to wait, to protect her.

Another anxious tap sounded on the door. "Merry? Are you still in there?"

"Be out in a minute." Merry tied a wide ribbon around her hair and opened the door to Janie's curious stare. "Were you worried?"

"Hmmph." Janie made no secret of her irritation. "You never tell me anything, Merry. It's not fair. I tell you—"

The phone rang, then. A clear, brassy intrusion. Janie turned toward the sound, but Merry stopped her. "Don't answer that. It's Emee."

Janie frowned at the plain black telephone. "How can you tell? It might be Ken."

"It's Emee. She's been calling the hotel and leaving messages for me. I should never have told her where I'd be staying."

"Why did you? You never tell her anything."

Merry stepped past Janie to rummage through the suitcase in search of sandals. "I don't know, Jane. When I visited her in Denver, she kept asking questions. Like she was really interested. Before I knew it, I'd told her my plans for this vacation. She even tried to insist on taking me to the airport. I had a heck of a time talking her out of that idea."

"What's with her?"

"I don't know. And I'm not about to answer the phone and find out, either. What if she wanted to join us?" Merry could think of few things that would so completely ruin a holiday. "Let's not talk about my mother. Let's go to the beach instead."

"Easy for you to say. Your bathing suit doesn't roll up on your thighs." With that, Janie closed the bathroom door and the phone stopped ringing.

THE SUN RODE LOW on the horizon, shooting the sky with one last blast of luxurious color. The ocean picked up the hue and reflected back a muted sunset. A slightly sunburned Molly darted ankle-deep into a wave, then jumped back, playing tag with the water and squealing with delight each time it oozed sand from beneath her toes.

"What energy." Lee commented from his seated position beside Merry. "Is she always like this?"

"Only when she's missed her afternoon nap. She'll sleep soundly tonight."

"As we all will."

"Janie probably was right to insist her girls rest for a while before dinner." From several feet away, Molly's delighted laughter echoed in the waning sunlight. "She's having so much fun."

"And vacations end so quickly."

Merry glanced at Lee and tried not to let her gaze linger on the browned expanse of his body. A fine mist of golden hair curled on his chest and broad shoulder muscles flexed with the movements of his hand sifting through a layer of sand. His bare legs, as tanned as the rest of him, created a bronze contrast against the cream-colored beach towel. He looked... *fine*, as Janie had said. Sensual, seductive. Every movement, every subtle motion he made whispered to Merry of tightly controlled desires. But last night she'd gotten a glimpse of passion that pushed past the boundaries of self-discipline and promised such sweet satisfaction. The memory wrapped into an unfamiliar, but recognizable longing inside her, and Merry forced herself to look away.

Lee had been quiet this afternoon, keeping his thoughts to himself. She'd wondered if he'd been uncomfortable with Ken's and Janie's effusive and often prying conversation or if Molly's presence had bothered him. But now, watching a slow smile tip the corners of his mouth as he observed Molly playing, Merry couldn't believe that was the problem. In fact, she couldn't imagine what was on his mind. He seemed distanced from her and the realization somehow frightened her.

"Janie isn't always so... talkative." Merry defended her friend because she liked Janie and she wanted Lee to like her, too. "I hope she didn't annoy you with all her questions."

"She was only trying to protect you." Lee lifted a handful of sand and let it drift away. "She's a good person to have on your side."

"I know, but there's no reason to take sides. It's not as if I needed protection. She acted as if you and I were ..." Merry looked away, but not before their eyes met for an instant of sharp awareness.

"As if you and I were what?" His voice deepened to a sexy baritone. "Lovers?" The word trembled between them and Merry ached with its possibilities.

"But we're not...."

Lee's dark eyes cornered her, challenged her to deny the attraction, the chemistry, if she could. "A technicality, Merry. You know it as well as I do. And as quick and curious as Janie is, she must have picked up on the vibrations, too." He leaned forward, cupping muscular arms around muscular legs. "She wants to make sure you're not going to get hurt."

"There's no need for her to worry."

It was a camouflaged plea for reassurance. Lee didn't need a doctoral degree to recognize that. He also knew he couldn't reassure her. What he had to say might hurt her. He thought she'd understand, but what if she didn't?

The idea knotted sickeningly inside him. He was an honest man and he'd never intended to deceive her. But somehow the situation had gotten out of his control. He had withheld information with only one other of the child stars he'd studied. And only then, because he'd felt it was necessary in order to clarify his findings. Whether or not it was necessary with Emerry, he'd never know. Circumstances had set up a scenario and with eyes open, he'd walked straight into it, until now he couldn't separate the part of him that wanted Emerry from the part that wanted Merry. And still, he had to tell her. He had to clear the air before it became too clouded with lies.

"Merry, there's something—"

Molly's cry cut through the sentence like a siren. In a split second, Lee was on his feet and racing ahead of Merry to reach the child. His heart pounding madly in his chest, he knelt in the wet sand and scanned Molly for signs of injury. A wave of relief washed over him when she pointed to a tiny cut on the bottom of her right foot. "I s-stepped on a shell." The words stuttered past quivering lips and two huge teardrops trembled on her eyelashes. She reached for her mother and in minutes, Merry had soothed the tears and cleaned the injury as best she could with the corner of her terry cover-up.

The moment was lost, though. Lee knew the explanation would have to wait again. At least for a few more hours. "Maybe we should get back to the hotel," he suggested. "She's going to need a Band-Aid and some antiseptic."

"Good idea," Merry said, lifting Molly into her arms. "If I know Ken and Janie, they'll be rested and ready to have dinner by the time we get back."

Molly protested about leaving the beach, but Merry insisted and Lee helped gather their things together for the walk back. By the time they reached the hotel, Molly had recovered and begged to be allowed to jump into the pool. Merry advised her to jump into the shower, instead, and Lee sympathized with a pouting Molly all the way up to the fourth floor.

"May I join you for dinner?" he asked when they reached Merry's room.

"Please." Merry's azure eyes smiled at him, seeking to understand his mood, searching for the answer to an unknown riddle.

He felt her insecurity, knew he was being unfair to her. "I didn't want to intrude," he said finally and, because he couldn't help himself, he touched her lips with his fingertip.

It was his undoing. Desire rose like steam inside him, hot and heady, interfering with his breathing, his heartbeat, his ability to think. She was like fine champagne, teasing his senses and whetting his appetite before he could even get a taste of her. His mouth moved slowly, inexorably toward hers. She lifted her chin, a sigh parting her lips—inviting . . . inviting.

"Mommy?"

Molly's tiny question brought them both to a crashing reality. This was hardly the time. Or the place. And yet they each knew the fire was gaining ground, forcing them toward the moment when it would catch and consume them.

"Yes," Merry said, but Lee wasn't certain if she was answering her daughter or him.

"I'll meet you downstairs." Lee lifted his finger again, but held it a fraction of an inch from her lips. Her breath warmed and moistened his skin and he could think of nothing except how badly he wanted to make love to her. "In an hour."

She nodded and, despite the nudge of Molly's hand on her fingers, she stood in the doorway, watching Lee, wanting Lee, and wondering how she could so quickly have lost herself in a pair of dark and mysterious eyes.

FOR MERRY, the evening passed in a glow of good friends, good food, and a secret anticipation. Lee's mood still eluded her. He conversed easily, surprising her with the range of interests and knowledge he possessed. During the afternoon, he and Ken had found a shared interest in computers and the various forms of software on the market and over dinner, they continued their discussion of the latest innovations and technology. Janie mentioned several times that the subject bored her and finally won the concession of lighter, more family-oriented conversation from the men. The girls picked at their dinners, asked innumerable questions about what they would do tomorrow, and begged for an opportunity to swim in the indoor pool.

Merry participated in the conversation, but was fully aware that her attention had settled elsewhere. She sensed a turmoil beneath the surface of Lee's calm, easy-going manner. *Lovers*, he had said. *A technicality.* The memory scorched her at moments, scared her at others. Last night they had come close, so close . . . Was it the thought of his body, naked and nestled with hers, that frightened and excited her? Was it something else? A threat, perhaps, that she could neither identify nor dismiss. Whatever Lee was thinking, whatever feelings he had, she couldn't begin to guess. But every time his eyes met her eyes or his hand brushed against her hand, indecision tumbled through her.

It was too late for them to become lovers. Merry was too conscious of Molly's watchful eyes and impressionable age. So why did she feel the seesaw tugs of maternal responsibility and sexual chemistry? It wasn't as if anything *could* happen now.

Yes, something happened with each glance. And each time, her indecision was overtaken by pure anticipation.

"Lee, would you watch us swim?" With uncanny intuition, Molly took her problem to the weakest link.

When Lee's mouth slanted in a pleased smile, Merry knew her daughter had scored a bull's-eye. "I'd love to." He turned to Merry. "You don't mind, do you? Ken and Janie can investigate the lounge while you and I chaperon these bathing beauties."

Three little girls giggled their pleasure and three parents knew they'd been outflanked. "You've just won a place in their hearts, Lee," Janie conceded. "At least until bedtime, which—" she checked her watch "—will be at nine-thirty. That gives you water nymphs thirty minutes to swim. Okay?"

"Okay!" The girls agreed eagerly and urged their mothers upstairs to help them change.

"I'll handle this," Janie said, motioning Merry back to her chair and taking Molly's hand along with Katy's. "You keep these men entertained until I return."

With a flurry of excited little-girl talk, they left. Merry smiled across the table at Lee. "It was thoughtful of you to volunteer."

"Volunteer?" Ken scoffed at the word. "Lee was doomed the moment Molly turned those big blue eyes in his direction. Honestly, Merry, she reminds me so much of you in those commer—"

Something in her expression must have warned him, because Ken broke off the words with a fit of coughing. "I think I'll run upstairs and change shoes. If I'm going to have to dance with Janie, I'd better have on my steel-toed boots."

With Ken gone, Lee studied the slight flush on Merry's cheeks. Had Ken's gaffe caused her high color? "Your daughter does look like you," Lee said. "She's a lucky young lady."

The blush subsided, delicately giving way to a soft, dusky shade of awareness. Had she been afraid he would pick up on what Ken had started to say? Had she worried that he would ask her if "commercials" was the interrupted word? Questions hovered on the fringes of his mind, waiting for the opportunity to probe the past, discover what had happened to Emerry Emilia Edwards. Was this the time to ask?

Lee pushed back from the table. "Let's stroll outside for a few minutes while we wait for the girls."

He seemed to take her agreement for granted, just as his handclasp discouraged protest. Merry's pulse picked up an extra beat as the formless threat stirred again just beyond her thoughts.

But outside, among the spiny-leaved plants and the heavy scent of flowers, her apprehension melted into an ache inside her. She wanted to kiss him. She wanted to be held in his arms. Only for a moment. Only until she could find again the sense of possibilities, of dreams not beyond her reach.

"Merry..." he began.

"Lee..." she said at the same moment. They turned, each toward the other, and suddenly words meant nothing. They reached for each other. It was as if neither of them had any other choice. When his lips touched hers, Merry thought she might never breathe again. If possession had been his intention, he accomplished it with little effort. She felt her reason splinter with his touch, knew she was losing control. Lee drew her close against him, although she hadn't thought she could be any closer. His hands slipped beneath the loose cotton top she wore and heat radiated outward from her spine and throughout her body. She was hot and trembling, afraid and excited, and indecisive.

As she struggled to conquer the intoxicating desire, the inexplicable need she had for this man, Merry realized that Lee was struggling, too. His breath seeped into her, even as he pulled his lips...reluctantly, so reluctantly...from hers. Beneath her palm, his heart pounded a message. She didn't know if she actually couldn't decipher it...or if she was afraid to do so.

"Merry, I—" The words stopped as he held her and stared into her eyes. The darkness shielded her vulnerability, she knew that, but in some fanciful corner of her mind, she thought he might see the passion glistening there. It seemed important, somehow, to hide it. She didn't want to spin out of control again.

A couple came toward them on the path from the street and Lee turned, sheltering Merry from their curious stares. "We'd better go inside," he said.

"I think you're right."

"Could you come for a walk with me later?" The words came out in a rush, as if he didn't want to consider them too long. "Would Janie watch Molly for you . . . for an hour or so?"

Merry knew she must refuse. Tonight something had changed. The tension between them spooled in waves of emotion over which she had no control. She could lose herself in Lee tonight . . . lose her reason, her heart. And she couldn't afford to do that. There were too many good reasons not to meet him later. The main one being Molly. "I . . . I can't, Lee. It's not fair to ask Janie to be away from her family. I'm sorry, I can't."

He brushed her cheek with the back of his hand. "I have to talk to you. Tonight. If we can't walk, then let me come to your room, after Molly's asleep. There are things about me you need to know before . . ."

Before? The word hung there. Fragile. Ambiguous. Provocative.

Merry swallowed hard, remembering last night, in her room, in his arms. "All right," she said. "You can come up. As soon as Molly's asleep."

7

"YOU COULD GO TO HIS ROOM." Janie pulled down the covers of the bed and stepped aside. "I'll stay here with Molly."

Merry shifted the sleeping child in her arms and lowered her to the bed. With tender movements, she tucked the sheets up to Molly's chin, even though she knew they'd be tossed off sometime during the night. "No, Janie. This is your vacation, too. I'm not going to impose upon your time with Ken."

"Impose away. Believe me, you need time with Lee more than I need time with my husband. I see Ken all the time."

Merry glanced up from the sweet picture Molly made. "Uh-huh. And almost every day at work, you complain about how family life intrudes upon romance. See, I listen more than you think I do."

Janie sighed and plopped, cross-legged, in the middle of the other bed. "Okay. So it's true that Ken and I have to make a special effort to spend time together. But we do get to sleep together every night and we have occasional weekends alone when my mother takes the girls. You, on the other hand, are never away from Molly. Even when your mother begs for time with Molly, you won't leave the two of them alone together for more than a few minutes. Take advantage of the opportunity, Merry. I'll sit right here. She'll never even know you're gone."

"No, Janie. I invited Lee to come here for a drink, if he wants. That way I'm here if Molly should awaken."

"Being here also removes any risk of anything exciting happening."

"I don't understand this sudden passionate interest in my sex life." Merry pulled one of the chairs out from the table and sat down, propping her stockinged feet up on the edge of the bed. "I mean, it's not as if it's any of your business."

"You're right, Merry. It isn't any of my business, but as your friend and mentor, I feel obliged to point out to you what you're missing. And I don't mean just sex, either. You're closing yourself into such a narrow little world, I'm afraid you'll never get out of it. It's you and Molly against the world and that's not good for either of you."

"We're doing just fine, Janie." Merry couldn't keep the defensiveness from her voice. "Just fine."

"Fine isn't good enough, Merry. There's more to life than going to work, going home, and tucking your child into bed."

Merry manufactured a polished, small, and insincere smile to hide her growing discomfort. "Don't say it, Janie. Don't use that trite and outdated line about how I need a man in my life."

"What you need is possibilities, Merry. And, deny it if you want, but Lee Zurbaron represents a whole realm of possibilities for you."

Merry leaned her head back, closed her eyes, and tried to pretend her heart wasn't echoing Janie's words. "Lee lives in California. In a couple of days, the possibilities he *supposedly* represents will be far out of reach."

"All the more reason to take advantage of them now. Quit pretending you're not head over heels infatuated with the guy and lose just a little bit of that rigid control you insist you have to have."

Molly stirred and turned over in her sleep and for a moment, silence shadowed the room. Merry wondered if Janie had any idea of what she was asking. Did she understand how much comfort could be found in that rigid control? Merry had lost it for a little while during the past couple of days and she didn't intend to lose it again. "Infatuation is nothing more than lust."

"And what's wrong with that? The air practically crackled tonight at dinner, Merry. And it wasn't because of the glances Ken and I exchanged. Whether it's lust, infatuation, or you're actually falling in love with Lee, something special is happening between the two of you. So, for heaven's sake, let me babysit Molly for a few hours while you try to figure out what it is."

"You're a good friend, Janie, but—"

"No buts, you're going." A shrill ring punctuated Janie's declaration. She glanced at the telephone. "That's Lee now. Tell him you'll meet him downstairs. No, no. In his room. That's better."

Ignoring Janie's chatter, Merry moved quickly to pick up the receiver before the phone could ring again. With a glance at Molly, still sleeping soundly, she spoke softly. "Hello?"

"Emerry. Hello, dear."

The sound of her mother's voice knotted Merry's stomach and set up a nervous tremor at the backs of her knees. "Hello, Emee," she said with no enthusiasm.

"How's my granddaughter? Is she there?"

"She's asleep."

"Oh, well, how's the vacation going?"

"Fine, thank you." Merry frowned and sat on the edge of the bed. Janie scooted over to make more room. Merry didn't have to look at her to know she was frowning, too. "Is something wrong?"

Emee's deep sigh was weary with unspoken wrongs. "I haven't felt too well since you left. My heart, again, I'm afraid. The doctor says I'm just lonely and dwelling on it...."

Merry tuned out the rest. Over the years, Emee's health had been as good or as bad as was necessary to manipulate the people in her life. But even now, when she should have built up an immunity to her mother's sympathy-seeking maneuvers, Merry felt a twinge of guilt. She didn't care, she insisted. She couldn't afford to care.

"I can't talk now," she said as soon as there was a break in the monologue. "I'll call you when I get home. Okay?" Merry hated adding the qualifier, hated herself for not being strong enough to stop herself. "I'll call next week."

"Oh, I see. That man is there."

Something in the hurried, exhilarated tone of her mother warned Merry even before the meaning of the words sunk in. An eerie sensation swirled around inside her. "What man? What are you talking about?" Merry asked.

There was a lengthy pause—Emee preparing her attack, Merry bracing for it. "Oh, you know, honey. That man who wanted to meet you. The psychologist. Has a funny name. Remember? I told you he'd come around asking questions about how to find you?"

Anger began to strangle the words before Merry could get them out. "But you didn't talk to him, Emee. You signed that contract. You agreed never to talk to anyone about me. That was the deal eight years ago. You got the money. I got privacy. Remember?"

"Of course, darling. I didn't talk to him. Except in the most general way. You know I would never break a promise to you."

Unless it suited your purpose, Merry thought. "Then why, Emee, did you think that he would be in my room—?" It struck her then. A psychologist. A funny name. Lee Zurbaron. Emee was talking about Lee.

Suffocating. She was suffocating. Blindly, she turned toward Janie, saw the questions and concern on her face, and yet saw nothing at all. Nothing, except Lee's eyes, his smile . . . his hand holding hers. "What did you tell him, Emee?" She tossed the accusation at her mother and wrestled with a faint hope that somehow she was wrong. *Lee. Emee.* No. Please.

"I did not tell him anything about you Emerry. I didn't." Emee's voice took on a familiar tone of authority, an "I-have-the-upper-hand" inflection. "But I've been worried about you. And the other night, after we had dinner together here in Denver, I was convinced I had to do something. You're getting too far away from your roots and, for your own good, I felt I had to step in."

How often had she heard that? Merry wondered. *For your own good.* What a lie. "What did you do?"

"Nothing that would alter our contract, dear." She sounded so pleased with herself, so sure what she had done was right. "I placed an anonymous call to the psychologist. He'd left me his card, you see. Told me to phone if I thought of anything that might be of interest to him. He's writing a dissertation on child stars. Doesn't that sound fascinating? And, of course, Emerry, you must be included. Why, as he said to me, you were America's darling. You were the biggest star of all." Emee paused, recalling, no doubt, the years of fame and fortune, the good years for her. "I knew you'd want to be included. Dissertations are often published, you know. In fact, I spoke to a publisher just yesterday who wants to talk with our psychologist." Emee breathed out a sigh of satisfaction. "I don't know why his name escapes me at the moment. He seemed like such a nice young man."

"Lee Zurbaron." Merry inserted the reminder flatly, her hope drowning in a numbing wave of betrayal.

"Yes, that's it. So he did find you. I wasn't sure. All I felt comfortable in saying was that you'd be on the flight from Denver to Houston. I figured he could take things from there." Emee paused. "And the call was anonymous, Emerry. He has no idea it came from me."

As if anonymity relieved her of responsibility. Merry shivered with fresh anger. "I could sue you for breach of contract, Emee."

"But you won't. I'm only doing this for you, Emerry. And for Molly. You know how much I love you both, how much I want to be a part of your lives, help you with—"

"No, Emee. You forfeited that right a long time ago. Molly and I don't need your help. And that includes anonymous calls and anything else you might think is for *our own good!*" With that, she slapped the receiver into the cradle and stood up. For a long time, all she could do was stare at the phone. Shaken, she walked to the window, parted the drapes and stared at the full glow of the moon. Then, she turned.

"Janie, would you stay here with Molly?"

"Sure. What's wrong?" Janie's eyes were wide, knowing enough to realize something was very wrong.

Merry felt the corners of her mouth lift in a cynical smile. "Nothing that can't be fixed."

"Does it have to do with Lee?"

"Yes." Merry heard her voice waver and brought up her chin to control it. She walked to the door before Janie could detain her with more questions. "Thanks, Janie. This won't take long."

"Take as long as you—"

Merry snapped the door behind her and, momentarily, sagged against it. But years of training, reinforced by a churning anger, stiffened her spine and propelled her. When was she going to learn her lesson? She had trusted Lee purely on instinct and had let herself be drawn to him by some primal sexual attraction. And look where that had gotten her. She should have known, should have seen her mistake. And yet, she'd sat there like an idiot, waiting for her mother to drop the bomb. Tears pushed at her eyelids, but she banished them through sheer force of will.

She would not cry, she told herself. Not now. Not later. Not ever. He wasn't worth it.

She found him downstairs, standing by the indoor pool where only a little while before they'd watched the girls swim. They'd sat side by side, not touching, except with a glance, a brush of fingertips across heated skin. She'd felt desired and desirable. If only she'd known then that he was looking at Emerry, not Merry. Never Merry.

"Lee." She walked up next to him. "Let's take a walk."

He turned and his eager smile drew the breath from her lungs. His gaze caressed her, burned her, evoked an emptiness inside her and a promise to fill it. But no. She reached into her past for a mask of composure.

"You changed your mind." He said it simply. Then, slowly, like a cloud passing the sun, he seemed to realize that something had happened. "Is Janie with Molly?" he asked, cautiously, tentatively,

"Yes." A couple pushed open the door and entered the lobby, laughing and talking. Merry wondered why their laughter sounded so hollow. "Will you walk with me?" she said to Lee.

"Of course. Where do you want to go?"

"It doesn't matter."

Lee regarded her with concern. "The beach?"

"That's fine."

She walked beside him in silence, drawing on every reserve she possessed to keep from screaming, *"Why?"* Shoulders straight, head high, she led the way. The tension held as they left the hotel grounds and crossed the boulevard to the seawall.

For reasons she wouldn't analyze, she avoided the sand and the surf, turning instead toward the rock jetty. The wind had picked up since the afternoon and it flirted outrageously with the folds of her skirt and teased tendrils of her hair. Merry controlled both with separate hands, as she turned to Lee and began.

"I just spoke to my mother, Lee."

He said nothing, as if waiting for the significance of her statement to emerge.

For a single second, Merry thought it might all turn out to be a mistake, a bad joke. "Emee mentioned that you'd been to see her. You were looking for me, I believe."

His jaw clenched. He looked down, brought a steady gaze to meet her accusing eyes. "I wanted to find Emery Edwards," he said.

"Congratulations. Your search is over. Isn't it an *amazing* coincidence that we should have been seated next to each other on the airplane." She strove for a light tone, but her voice sounded uneven, shaken. She hardly recognized it as her own. "It's a small world, isn't it, Lee?"

"Sarcasm doesn't suit you, Merry."

"I agree. But it seems so appropriate. You see, a recent experience has left me somewhat cynical."

"Don't make this into something it isn't." His inflection warned her, the set of his jaw challenged her to fight fairly. "At least, give me a chance to explain."

"I'm not interested in explanations, Lee, but I would like to know what it is you want from me."

"Let's begin by getting out of this wind and finding a more comfortable place to talk."

Merry tossed her head, freeing her hair to the caprice of the wind and the spray of the waves. "This isn't going to be comfortable, Lee, no matter where we go. Just get it over with."

He ran nervous fingers through his hair and frowned at the horizon for moments that stretched to infinity. "All right. I'm a psychologist and for my doctoral study I chose to research child stars and the effects of fame on their later lives. I've been working on it for almost two years now, interviewing people, researching background, anything pertaining to the subject of famous children who became famous or, more often, non-famous adults."

"And did you lie to all of them, too?"

"I didn't lie to you."

"You didn't tell the truth, either, Lee."

"There wasn't an opportunity."

"You didn't make one, you mean."

"All right. I didn't make one. And for that, I apologize. There, is that what you wanted?"

"No. I wanted you to be real. I wanted you to be a hero." Her lower lip almost trembled, but she caught it in time. "Goodbye, Lee."

She moved to walk past him, but he grabbed her arm and stopped her. "What do you mean, *goodbye?* Aren't you going to give me a chance to explain? Does our relationship mean nothing to you?"

"Relationships are for people who trust each other, Lee. You used me. You used my emotions. And if I let you, you'd exploit my past for your own gain."

"That isn't true."

Merry shrugged. "It doesn't matter."

"No, you're wrong. It matters a hell of a lot. I'm not trying to exploit you. I'm trying to understand you. I came looking for Emerry. I admit that. I wanted to talk to her, find out why she'd dropped out of an eighteen-year career, disappeared presumably from the face of the earth. But I found *you*, instead. And I wanted to get to know you. I wanted to understand how Emerry came to be Merry and why."

"You might have asked, Lee."

"You wouldn't have let me get any closer if I had."

"Probably not. But at least you wouldn't have lied."

"Merry, I—"

"No, please. Don't say any more. And don't bother me again."

"But you haven't—"

"Look, I've heard every line in the book...and I'm just not interested in hearing yours." She had no more energy left, no more emotion. Emptiness was all she felt and she took the first painful steps away from him.

"Emerry."

The name washed over her with years of memories, some good, some not, but it was the way Lee said it that stopped her. "Emerry no longer exists," she said before she walked on, determined not to look back.

"If that's so," Lee called above the ocean noise, "why are you still running away from her?"

She kept going and as he stared at her straight, unyielding back, he knew it wouldn't do any good to go after her. Merry, Emerry, whatever she called herself, wasn't in any mood to listen to him. She had anointed herself judge and jury and had convicted him without a hearing. But what bothered him the most was that he understood why she'd done it.

Merry had left him on the pier with a multitude of words unsaid, because it was easier to walk away from him than to face her past and decide who she really was.

MERRY REACHED HER ROOM without being aware of the journey. She glossed over the incident for Janie, leaving the impression it was nothing more than a disagreement, a misunderstanding, being careful to show more anger than hurt, more annoyance than injury.

Janie offered sympathy, but Merry wanted none. She knew Janie hadn't had much experience with people like Lee and Emee. People who exploited others for personal satisfaction. Merry hated it. She hated herself for having been weak enough to fall for another line. She hated Lee for making her think, if only for a day, that love might be possible.

After Janie left, Merry checked Molly, tucking the covers once again around the tiny shoulders. She wandered to the window and in passing, noticed the carafe and wineglasses she'd ordered earlier that evening. If she'd been alone, Merry thought she might have swept them from the table with a strong backhand. Instead, she carried the carafe to the bathroom and poured out the wine, watching until every last drop swirled down the drain. Then she set the tray with the empty bottle and unused glasses outside her door.

One reminder of Lee disposed of.

Only another few memories to go.

She pulled one of the chairs close to the window, parted the drapes and turned out the lights. The moon cut a lazy path across the sky, frosting the night with a silver glow. The tide swirled in dark ribbons along the beach, coming in, going out. She could see people walking there, pale shadows moving through the night and along her line of vision. Traffic lights blinked nearer the hotel, stopping and releasing cars with soothing monotony.

Merry watched the scene for endless minutes, forcing her thoughts into strict channels of meaningless observation. It was a trick she'd learned, this disciplining of her mind. It had helped her withstand the strain of long hours under hot lights when she was modeling.

Come on, baby, one more. Yeah, that's it. Now, a little smile . . . not too much. One more time. The words came to her through a time tunnel, the voice indistinguishable, but familiar. Any number of photographers had said the same things to her. *Smile. Turn. Give me that look.* And she had smiled, turned, changed expression on cue. All because she was in control. Emee had taught her that much.

Once she'd been sick with a fever, but Emee had insisted she could manage for one day. The commercial was already over budget and pushing the deadline. So she'd dosed Merry with aspirin, powdered out the flush on her cheeks and posed her in front of the camera. "Shine, honey," she'd said and from somewhere, Merry had found the energy to "shine."

There'd been other times, too. Times when she'd been so weary of being a child in an adult world that she'd cried for the privilege of play. Emee always promised that tomorrow or the next day she could play. She could have friends over, toys, anything she wanted. But today she had to work. They needed the money. The contract couldn't be broken today.

Tomorrow, of course, never came. Emerry had no friends and no time to play with the innumerable toys in her room. But she couldn't complain. Why, she was America's darling! Emee reminded her every day of how lucky she was, of how many little girls longed to be Emerry Emilia Edwards, the Hamil and Harrison Companies' Little Miss Sunshine. Every night Emee tucked her into bed with a kiss on the forehead and a whispered, "Doesn't it feel wonderful to be a star?"

It felt lonely. She might as well have been King Midas's daughter, changed from a princess into a statue of gold by a "loving," parental touch.

Molly sighed and Merry's gaze sought her huddled form on the bed. Emee wasn't going to touch Molly's life with her dreams of fame and fortune. Ever since Molly's birth, Emee had been behaving like a real grandmother, a real person. At times, Merry had actually considered the idea that her mother might be changing. But then, always, Emee would bring up Molly's career, how Molly should be taking her place in the world. And Merry wouldn't have that. If she had to, she could forbid Emee to see her granddaughter. And if push came to shove, she would.

A small, insistent voice whispered that Emee was who she was, that she meant no harm. She simply didn't know how to be a conventional mother...or grandmother. She craved the spotlight and it was inconceivable to her that Merry wanted no part of it. She saw her daughter's abdication as a rebellious phase, one she'd eventually regret.

Merry had given up trying to make her understand.

And she certainly wasn't going to open up her reasons for Lee to analyze.

Lee.

The hurt came in a rush and she was unprepared for its force. She was determined not to cry, but as the moonlight made a slow arc across the sky, she wondered if it might not have been easier.

Being in control was sometimes so damn lonely.

8

MERRY AWAKENED with Molly in her lap, asleep against her shoulder. The two of them were nestled into the contours of the chair, draped into a half-sitting, half-reclining posture. With a flex of her arm, Merry shifted her daughter and smoothed the dark hair from her baby-soft cheeks.

Molly pursed her lips in a pouty frown before settling into her mother's embrace. She had Ian's mouth, Merry thought with some pride. The full lips, the promise of a dimple at one corner, and the set of her chin were all reminiscent of Ian. But in all other ways, she favored Merry. Emee loved to remark upon the resemblance. And the possibilities for marketing that resemblance.

With a steady hand, Merry swept her fingers through her own hair and turned her face toward the window and the sunrise. Although the first shades of dawn were just now changing into gold on the horizon, she could still make out a solitary figure on the beach. A shell seeker, she thought. Chasing the tide for treasure.

Merry watched, but the shell seeker didn't follow the path of the water on the sand, didn't appear to be looking for shells at all. The man—for the build was too broad to belong to a woman—stood, hands in pockets, staring out to sea. Maybe the early morning beachcomber had wanted to see the sunrise over the Gulf of Mexico. It could be that simple.

For several minutes, Merry stared, wondering if it was Lee. But when he made a turn, walked a few steps toward the pier and then out onto the jetty, she knew. From her window, she could see well enough to observe the sea gulls landing on the beach and the blur that indicated a freighter far out in the gulf. She couldn't be sure of anyone's identity from this distance, and yet something in the man's movements—a sense of loneliness, perhaps—spoke to her.

Lee.

Had he slept well? Or at all? What were his thoughts on this fresh morning when Galveston had lost its romantic glow? Was he disappointed that he had followed her here only to be rejected? Or was he plotting some other means of getting past her to reach the Sunshine Girl?

Molly made a soft mewling sound and her blue eyes blinked open. She yawned into Merry's shoulder, then burrowed deeper into motherly arms.

"Good morning." Merry greeted her daughter by kissing the top of her head. "Are you warm enough?"

The small head bobbed up and down. "Can we swim?"

"Swim? It seems very early for swimming, Miss Molly Grace." Merry stroked Molly's round cheeks. "Didn't you get enough swimming last night?"

"No," came the swift and honest reply. "Willie didn't neither."

"Is that right?"

Molly nodded solemnly. "Please?"

"Maybe after breakfast, when Carol and Katy are—"

"No, Mommy. Just me 'n Willie. And you."

How could she resist such a plea? Merry wondered. Molly excelled at manipulating her maternal weak spots. "I don't think I'm ready to plunge into the ocean, Molly.

But I suppose we might look for some shells. Would you like that?"

Bright blue eyes shone from the pixie face, as Molly sat upright and offered an eager nod. "Can I wear my bikini?"

"You might get cold."

"I won't, Mommy. 'Kay?"

Merry gave in reluctantly. "Take your cover-up."

Molly was on her feet in a flash, scampering across the floor and digging through her bag to find the bright green, polka dot swimsuit. Merry glanced back at the figure on the beach. He was far out on the jetty now, a solitary silhouette against the dawn. A subtle yearning stirred inside her, born of loneliness, nourished by too many wistful dreams. If only for a moment, she had found something indefinably special with Lee and her heart clung to the foolish belief *he* was somehow different from other men.

He wasn't, of course. While still in her teens, she'd been deceived by more accomplished actors than Lee Zurbaron. Any lingering emotion was simply wishful thinking on her part and would be gone in a day or so. And if she ran into him on the beach this morning? Well . . .

Merry rose to assist Molly with her swimsuit and to change into something less "slept in." Lee wouldn't speak to her, she decided. She'd made it crystal clear last night that she didn't wish to hear anything he had to say. And if he insisted, she would give him a cool dismissal. Nothing more.

"Ready, Mommy? Ready?" Molly hopped around the room, making flip-flopping noises with her sandals. "Let's go."

"I'm ready, sweetheart." She led the way to the door, thinking, *hoping*, she was ready for anything.

LEE SAW MOLLY FIRST, but his glance went quickly past her, searching for Merry. She wore a black one-piece jumpsuit beneath a blue net jacket, a wide-brimmed hat, and dark sunglasses. It was a subtle disguise, Lee thought, and wondered if her subconscious intent was to hide from the general public...or from him. He thrust one hand into the hip pocket of his khaki shorts as he watched their progress down the seawall. Then, with studied determination, he took a couple of steps toward them and waited for Molly to notice his presence.

"Lee!" She waved a happy greeting. "We're hunt'n shells!" Without waiting for her mother, Molly broke into a short-legged run. Her smile reminded him of Merry in at least a dozen childhood photographs. Lee realized anew the unique difficulties Merry faced in raising her daughter outside the shadow of her own success. It wouldn't get easier, either, he thought as he bent down to receive the hug Molly offered. She giggled and wiggled as he squeezed her briefly in a sincerely affectionate hug. How could anyone resist this charming bundle of sunshine? Certainly not he. He'd fallen almost as hard for the daughter as he had for her mother.

"Hello, Lee."

At Merry's words, he looked up, prepared by the crisply polite voice for her unwelcoming expression. Although he recognized the cool facade for the fragile pretense it was, hurt coiled in his heart. "Good morning, Merry." He knew there was only one way to play this scene and that was straight out. "Are you hunting seashells, too?"

"Yes." She turned to Molly, intentionally shutting him out. "Let's check the tide pools, Molly. Maybe we'll see something interesting there."

The child nodded eagerly and slipped one hand into her mother's hand and the other hand, quite innocently, into Lee's. "Come on, Lee."

"I'm sure Mr.—Lee has other things to do, Molly."

Her control was wearing a little thin, Lee thought, and he was grateful for Molly's trusting presence. Merry would not be rude to him in front of her daughter. No matter how uncomfortable the situation, she would not involve Molly in a scene. It might be unfair, but Lee knew he was going to take full advantage of the fact. "I didn't think to check the tide pools," he said. "Let's do that."

They tracked the path of the tide, Molly jumping and chatting with her imaginary friend, while the tension stretched taut above her head. When they found one of the pools, Lee went down on both knees to explore the ocean treasures with Molly. Merry sat on a rock and sifted through the captive water for an interesting shell, but she said little and never once made any comment to Lee or in any way acknowledged him. When he saw the sand dollar, he knew luck was on his side.

"Look, Molly." His voice deepened with wonder. "Look at this shell."

Molly leaned in to see and breathed out a sigh of pure delight, although Lee was certain she had no idea what he held. She lifted it from his palm and turned the round shell over and over in her fingers, her mouth forming a tiny "oh" of pleasure. "Pretty," she said.

"It's a sand dollar," Lee explained. "And they're not easy to find. This must be a special day for you."

Bright blue eyes flicked to his, then back to the prized sand dollar. "Lucky." She agreed simply. "Look, Mommy. A sand doll."

"Dollar." Merry corrected the child. "But it's not like a dollar you can spend. It's a special kind of shell with five tiny pieces inside. The pieces are shaped like birds. People tell stories about the shell, too, and think it is very special."

Molly seemed pleased by that information. "More. Willie wants one." She turned back to the pool and began splashing at the water.

"There's not likely to be another one in there, Molly." Merry smoothed the wayward strand of hair that swung down across Molly's forehead. "Sand dollars are hard to find. Especially whole ones. You might find some smaller pieces along the beach, though."

Molly glanced at the stretch of sand and jumped up. "I look," she said.

"Stay close," Merry warned. "And don't go into the water, okay?"

"'Kay." Molly was off like a shot with the sand dollar clutched in her fist.

Alone with Merry, Lee let the silence build for a moment or two. He sensed her discomfort, despite the care she took to hide it. He was uncomfortable, too, and fought against a crazy impulse to tell her she'd made a terrible mistake. He didn't know anything about her past, had never met her mother, and had no interest whatsoever in a young model named Emerry Edwards.

But the truth was, he did know. And even if he could forget Emerry, even if he could throw out the years he'd spent on his dissertation, it wouldn't do any good. Not unless Merry could forget, too. And Lee had too much training to think that was possible. Sooner or later, Merry would have to face her past. Like it or not.

"Did you sleep at all last night?" He tossed out the question as an opener, something to show her he wasn't going to disappear because she wanted him to.

"Fine, thank you."

A rueful smile tugged at the corner of his mouth. "I hardly slept, either. I've been on the beach since five o'clock this morning."

"Then perhaps you should go back to the hotel. There's no need to stay for Molly's benefit."

"I'm not staying for Molly's benefit. You and I have things to discuss."

That made her angry. He watched her struggle for control over the hot words he suspected weighed heavily on her tongue. Control won.

"I have nothing to say to you, Lee."

"You have so much to say it's eating away inside you."

A crisp silence permeated the open air. Lee hoped she was angry. He wanted her angry enough to talk to him.

"You're mistaken." She kept her gaze fixed on Molly. The sunglasses shielded her eyes from his watchful gaze, but he knew he'd struck a nerve.

Lee pulled his hand from the water and clasped his arms around his bent knees. The hem of his khaki shorts rode high, revealing an expanse of muscled thigh and leg hair tanned golden by the sun. His pose was relaxed, friendly, but the tight play of muscles across the back of his neck belied it. "I'm not going away, Merry."

"Suit yourself," she said, while every corner of her heart cried out for him to stay. As if it mattered, as if she could simply forgive him for not being the man she'd believed him to be. She should be angry, furious, so irate she could walk away from him without a second thought. Her hand trembled, but she buried it in her jacket pocket. She would get up, leave him and his memory behind. But she continued to sit, unable to initiate any action at all, frozen in a numbing vacuum of immobility. "Molly," she called. "Don't get too far away."

"I could say the same thing to you." Lee spoke softly into the ensuing quiet. "Don't get too far away from me, Merry."

Her chin swung toward him, her gaze—behind the sunglasses—locked with his, and her lips became taut with suppressed anger. "You have no right to talk to me like that. Not after what you've done."

"And just what is that?"

Ooh, he was smug. Thinking he could draw her out with the right combination of words and that wounded and tender note in his voice. "Games are for children, Lee. Leave me alone."

"I don't think I can. Maybe there was a point where I could have, but not now. Not after... Not after the memories we've made together."

She didn't want to be reminded, didn't want to believe they'd shared anything at all. "Those memories are a lie, Lee. You spoiled them."

He turned his head, staring at either Molly or the ocean, she couldn't tell which. His silence frightened her in a way, but she told herself she was misreading her feelings. It would be crazy to keep talking with him, as if she *wanted* him to explain. She wanted silence. She wanted Lee to go away.

He sat too close to her. His arms clasped his bare knees with latent strength. The muscles of his calves flexed powerfully whenever he made a slight shift in position. Last night's beard shadowed his jawline and Merry had a sudden, nearly irresistible impulse to touch it, to know the textures of his face in the early morning. Resisting it caused a turmoil of sensations inside her, brought her fingers curling into her palm. Stupid thoughts. Silly longings. She knew better.

Damn it, she *knew* better.

"I'm sorry you've allowed my dissertation to cancel out the pleasures of the past couple of days, Merry."

Lee's voice startled her out of her private thoughts. "It's not your 'dissertation', Lee. It's the way you lied about it."

"And you've decided I'm guilty without bothering to hear my side of the story."

Merry bit back a pithy contradiction and lifted her shoulder in what she hoped was an indifferent shrug. "Life isn't fair, Lee. You should know that."

"I'm beginning to see just how unfair it can be, thanks to you."

"You chose the scenario, Lee, not me."

For a moment, she thought he would argue, try to deny his deception and its consequences. When he did speak, though, no hint of contentiousness could be discerned in his voice. "I believe you really want to talk, Merry. I think you wish I could somehow force you to listen to me." His dark gaze lay heavily on her, willing her to look into his eyes and see the truth.

She felt the pressure, but refused to give in and turn toward him. "All I want is to be left alone."

"Well, I think you're lying." His voice wore a hint of a smile, a slight tone of conciliation. "So, Merry, here we are with one 'supposed' lie apiece. What do we do now?"

"I'm going to get my daughter and go back to the hotel. You do whatever you wish."

"Thank you. I intend to." He rose, dusting sand from his legs and hips.

Unbidden, her gaze followed his movements, taking in every detail of his physique, every sensual motion he made. Merry tried to control her anger, tried to ignore the response spiraling through her, but it made steady and compelling progress despite her efforts. In desperation, she stood, jerked her glance to her daughter and followed it with determined footsteps. She felt a mix of both irritation and dismay when Lee fell into step beside her.

"Mommy, look." Molly pointed proudly to a mound of shells, some broken, some whole, all dirty.

Lee bent to examine them with a critical eye. "You're a real treasure hunter, Molly. There must be a couple of dozen shells here."

"Let's wash them before we take them to the hotel room." Merry picked out the choicer bits of seashell and carried them to the edge of the water where she rinsed them and let them drip dry in her hand. A nerve at the back of her neck tingled a warning just before Lee knelt next to her, his big hands filled with shells. Side by side, companionably, as if the air between them wasn't burdened with unspoken emotions, they rinsed Molly's shells in the shallow water.

"You carry them, Mommy." Molly's voice came over Merry's shoulder. "My hand's too small."

"I can put some in my pocket." Merry indicated the pocket on her net jacket and Molly put her hand inside to inspect it.

"Holes," she announced solemnly. "You have a pocket?" she asked Lee.

"I have a shoe. Two, in fact. Would you like to borrow them?" His dark eyes sparkled with amusement as Molly glanced in wonder at his feet, her dimpled smile showing fascination with his suggestion.

She bent to grab one and fell forward into the water. Lee caught her before the next ripple of tide could reach her and soon had her laughing. "Molly Mermaid," he called her and she replied with a delighted giggle.

Merry watched the two of them and wanted both to wrench Molly away from him and to laugh with them. Torn between two actions, neither of which she would consider doing because of the possible effect on Molly, she forced her attention to the shells and the washing of their shiny surfaces. When Lee had taken off his shoes— an unscuffed pair of boondockers—and helped Molly tuck her treasures inside them, he turned to Merry. "Would you like to carry this?" he asked, offering her one of the shoes.

The gesture was simple, hardly one of profound symbolism and yet Merry's heart pounded as if he were giving her something of immeasurable value. Her control slipped slightly as her eyes made contact with his. She grappled to recover it, to maintain the comforting façade of indifference as she accepted the shoe filled with shells and held it just below her breast.

Lee followed the movement with his gaze and a sudden heat swirled through her and around her. She took a deep, cleansing, calming breath and wondered why it was so hard to maintain a justifiable anger. "Come on, Molly." She pushed aside the question and offered her hand to Molly. But Molly had both hands full with Lee's other shoe and Merry's fingers brushed through air, until Lee placed his hand around hers.

She flinched and a shell spilled onto the sand. Lee stooped to retrieve it and Merry made a last attempt to exhibit indifference. When he straightened up, her hand was safely again at her side.

Lee walked ahead with Molly, his stride shortened to match hers. He gave no indication that the abbreviated pace was uncomfortable or that he felt the occasional jab of a sharp rock against his bare feet. Merry trailed a few

steps behind as they climbed the stairs and as they waited
for a break in traffic before crossing the street.

The threesome entered the hotel lobby in the same
fashion—Molly in the lead with Lee stepping ahead to
open doors and waiting for Merry to walk through. She'd
decided she would accept Lee's help only until they
reached their room. For Molly's sake, she could manage
that. But then she would make it clear—

"We were wondering where you were." The Lesters, all
four, stepped from the arriving elevator. The girls began
talking as Molly showed off her treasure. Merry saw the
flash of curiosity in Janie's eyes immediately and knew a
second later that her friend had misread the situation.
"Lee," Janie said with a smile. "Good to see you this
morning. We're going for breakfast. Ken's starving as
usual. Why don't you join us?"

A protest lodged in Merry's throat as Ken heartily en-
dorsed the idea. "You know, Lee, I wanted another
chance to ask you about that computer software we dis-
cussed last night. I was thinking..." He broke off. "Were
you on your way up?"

"Well . . ." Lee looked at Merry, saw her distress and
made his decision. He couldn't afford to be intimidated
by her anger. No matter how many times she asked, he
wasn't going to quietly walk out of her life. The way it
looked, Lee thought, he couldn't possibly make the situation any worse by accepting the invitation. "I'm sure
Molly can handle the treasure with her mother's help."

Once again, anger sparked an azure gleam in Merry's
eyes and Lee felt vindicated. She needed to be angry, to
release some of her pent-up emotion. She needed it badly.

Merry guided Molly into the elevator without a word.

"You'll be down in a minute, won't you?" Janie asked,
but the answer, if there was one, disappeared with the

ascending elevator. "What have you two been doing?" Janie turned her curiosity to Lee.

"Searching for shells on the beach." Lee's tone was noncommittal, his smile reassuring. "Molly found a sand dollar."

"And it looks like you lost your shoes." Janie teased him with a friendly smile and Lee realized she thought he and Merry had made up . . . if Janie knew about the quarrel at all.

He glanced at his bare feet, wondering if Janie would be his ally in the quest to win back Merry's trust. "I'd forgotten," he said. "I'll go up and get another pair."

"Should we save you a place at our table?" Janie asked.

Lee hesitated, weighing his decision one last time against Merry's disapproval. "Yes," he answered. "I'll be right back." With that, he walked barefoot up the stairs to his floor.

On his way back, he thought about stopping by Merry's room, but decided that would only give her the opportunity—again—to ask him to leave her alone. And, Lee decided, he'd rather she did that in front of witnesses. He didn't think she'd mention her problems within the confines of a group, but if she did, she'd have to offer some explanation and that, after all, was what he wanted. If she had to put his alleged deception in words and voice it to an outside party, she'd *have* to see his side of the situation. At least, in theory. She might not like it any better, but it would certainly give him more ground for argument.

Ken and Janie were moving through the buffet line when Lee entered the restaurant. They motioned him to the round table where Carol and Katy sat. The girls welcomed him by asking when he would find a sand dollar for them. He explained the difficulty as best he could and silently vowed to buy two sand dollars in the gift shop and "discover" them on the beach later that day. When Janie and Ken returned, the discussion on sand dollars continued and gradually evolved into a conversation about Galveston and other vacation spots in Texas.

Several times during the meal Janie wondered aloud whether or not she should check on Merry and Molly. Lee suspected Merry was having a slight problem with her image and he knew she wouldn't face him again without having her mask of composure firmly in place. He didn't say so, of course, but he couldn't keep his glance from straying to the lobby to search for her.

Just when he'd decided she wasn't going to come back downstairs, she and Molly entered the room and approached the table. "Sorry we took so long. I wanted to wash Molly's hair."

The excuse was genuine—Molly's dark hair shimmered with highlights and bounce. Merry's hair looked as if it had been washed, too, but she had it caught back from her face in two wide clips and the bounce as well as the highlights were subdued. She'd changed clothes, too. Now she wore a vivid sundress of pink and turquoise, fitted at the bodice, flared at the hips.

Lee caught his breath at the sheer elegance she projected and didn't understand why every eye in the place wasn't on her. He couldn't seem to force his away.

His steady regard accomplished in a moment what Merry had been trying to do with a stern mental lecture. It balanced her. She'd been struggling with what to do, what to say, when she reached the table, but now suddenly, she knew. Lee had hurt her. He'd deceived her and for that, she would not forgive him. But she'd be a fool not to recognize the scintillating attraction still at work between them. It didn't matter, but at least she knew where to fortify her defenses. And she would not, under any circumstances, give him the satisfaction of knowing how deeply he'd hurt her.

Seating Molly first and then herself, Merry smiled at the expectant little group. "Should we order or try the buffet?" she asked pleasantly, avoiding the slightest glance in Lee's direction. "The fruit looks good."

"It is," Janie said and the mood of the day was set. Merry hoped so, anyway. She'd done her part, made the decision to put up a front for the benefit of her daughter and her friends. Vacations didn't come along so often that she could afford to spoil even one. If Lee insisted on tagging along, pretending nothing was wrong, then so be it. She'd survived more difficult assignments.

It required more effort than she'd expected, but Merry made it through the day of swimming, sunning and shopping. Lee, more often than not, was by her side...at a discreet distance, of course. She spoke to him only when absolutely necessary and never allowed her gaze to linger on him for more than a glance. She didn't think Janie or Ken noticed anything was amiss, but wasn't overly concerned one way or the other. The message she wanted to give was for Lee alone.

He received it loud and clear...and made up his mind to overlook it. At some moment, maybe on the airplane, maybe later, maybe even before he'd met her, he'd gone beyond professional involvement with her. It was time now to recoup some of that lost perspective, if he could. Although he'd hurt Merry unintentionally, it would take patience and persistence to win back her trust.

A worthy goal, he thought, and not unattainable. He'd faced more difficult cases and found a way to break down the psychological barriers. He could do it again. He'd just have to be careful not to sacrifice his professional goals for personal ones.

And vice versa.

He only hoped he could do all of this without completely losing his heart.

By the end of the day, though, Lee wasn't sure he had much heart left to lose. Merry, for all her cool facade, captivated him. Her laughter warmed him and brought a smile winging to his lips. Her voice, low and husky, though never directed to him, had him leaning toward her to hear what she had to say. Anything, everything, she had to say.

He waited for an opportunity to be alone with her, but when it came, he was caught off-guard.

"How about a game of Candyland in our room as soon as you girls are washed and squeaky clean?" Janie suggested to Carol, Katy and Molly after they'd all watched the sunset from the end of the pier. Three sunburned noses wrinkled in indecision before the girls decided bath, bed and a board game was the best offer they could expect on their last night in town.

"Can we take a bath together?" Carol phrased the counter-offer. "Molly, too?"

"With our seashells?" Molly added, clutching her new sand-pail and shovel.

Janie grimaced, but gave in under the collective argument of the girls, aided and abetted by Ken. When the question arose as to which adult would oversee the proposed bath and which one would make the fourth player in Candyland, Lee settled the matter. "You and Ken take the girls back to the hotel, Janie. I'll gather up the picnic stuff and bring it along in a few minutes." He glanced at Merry. "Will you stay and help?"

Merry hardly hesitated. "Sure," she said. "Why not?"

Her agreement took Lee by surprise. He'd expected an excuse, a rash of reasons why she had to accompany Molly and the Lesters to the hotel. He hadn't dared to hope she might actually stay.

"You don't mind, do you, Janie?" Merry asked her friend, making sure the arrangements for Molly were not an imposition. "I'll come to your room as soon as Lee and I are finished."

Lee caught the implication even as Janie assured Merry there was no need to hurry. *Finished.* So this was to be the last curtain, he thought as he helped the Lesters gather the girls and their belongings. Merry intended to give him a final goodbye. A small, rueful frown settled on his lips.

"Goodnight, girls," he called as the five walked away. "Goodnight, Molly. See you in the morning."

"See you." Molly waved her bucket in reply and then, for all practical purposes, he and Merry were alone on the beach at twilight.

"We're leaving in the morning." Merry turned immediately to the picnic cloth and dropped to her knees in the sand. She began clearing the remains of the supper they'd all shared. "Early."

"That's all right. I'll be there to say—"

"There's no need. You and I are saying goodbye right now, Lee."

"We are?"

She tossed a plastic fork on the middle of the checkered cloth, followed by a second and a third. "I told you last night that I wished to be left alone. You chose to disregard my request and, because I didn't want to create a scene, I allowed you to infringe upon my vacation for the day. But the day's ended, the vacation is over. So, goodbye."

Lee walked over and plopped onto the corner of the checkered cloth, near enough to arrest her gaze, close enough to touch... if she'd wanted to touch him. She didn't. She wadded a napkin into a tight ball and looked for a sack to throw it into.

"Have you been practicing that speech all day, Merry?" Lee asked quietly. "And did you really think that after you'd said it, I'd just walk away without a protest?"

She glanced at him, knew immediately she'd made a mistake, but couldn't look away then from his dark, penetrating eyes. "I hoped you might." Her whisper barely disturbed the calm evening air and still he wouldn't release her from his gaze.

"I don't think you hoped that at all, Merry."

For the space of a dozen heartbeats or more, she hung suspended between how she knew she ought to feel and the feelings actually running rampant through her. Something happened to her when she was with Lee. Something that was beyond her control. Something she couldn't, or wouldn't, explain. She trembled with awareness, with a warm need to disregard all she knew of logic and trust and betrayal and give herself unreservedly to this man. Without doubt or question.

It was nonsense, of course. Emotions could be so irrational, so untrustworthy. She broke the sustained gaze and began gathering up the corners of the cloth...all but one corner. "I have one more thing to say to you, Lee. I can't stop you from writing a book, but if you put anything about me in it... anything at all... I'll sue."

Lee shifted off the cloth and pulled up the corner to match the three she held. His knees indented the sand close, very close, to where she knelt. One muscular and sandy thigh brushed against her leg and the inadvertent contact sparked heated fire in her belly. His hands closed over hers purposefully before she realized his intention, but she didn't struggle or jerk away. That, she told herself, would be undignified.

She could stand the scintillating touch of his hands; she could bear the sensuous feel of his skin against her leg . . . for a few seconds, maybe longer. She wasn't sure, though, if she could go without breathing that long.

"First off, Merry—" Lee's voice was tight, his expression intense as he leaned toward her "—I'm writing a dissertation, not a book. And secondly, you can sue me if you want, but let's get something straight right here and now. What I write or don't write is not the problem. You're afraid of the way I feel about you. You're afraid of the way you feel about me. But most of all, you're afraid I might be a little more in love with Emerry than with Merry. And you can't allow yourself to take that chance."

A little more in love, he'd said. But he didn't mean it. How could he mean it? There was no joy in the short laugh she forced from her dry throat. "And you're afraid you won't get the information you need to finish your dissertation. Well, easy come, easy go, Mr. Zurbaron. And I *am* going." She started to rise, and he rose with her. The picnic cloth dangled its bounty between them. "Let go of my hands," she said.

"I will, in a moment. Just as soon as you understand my position."

"Your *position?*" She made the taunt a challenge, even though her heart thundered in surrender against her chest.

"I didn't lie to you, Merry. Maybe I didn't handle the situation properly, but any deception on my part was created by a set of circumstances neither of us could have predicted or controlled. Why can't you accept that I mean you no harm, not in the dissertation and not in any other way? I am not a threat to you, your daughter, or your happiness."

Oh, but he was. He was. "Words don't make everything all right, Lee. There are some things I can't give, and some things I can't forgive."

His hold on her slackened. Exasperation or anger or maybe some other kind of emotion shadowed his eyes in the deepening twilight. "Oh, I see. I've asked for something you can't give and in doing so, I've done something you can't forgive." His hands dropped from hers. "Is that it, Merry?"

Why did he make this so hard? "Yes," she said flatly. "That's it. Now, will you leave me alone?"

He shifted the cloth and its contents in his hands and turned away from her. After looking around the area, he motioned her to precede him across the sand. Merry complied because there was no other path available to her. To run from his presence as she longed to do would be to lose control so completely that he would know the hurt he'd caused her. And she didn't want him to know. Not ever.

The walk to the hotel and the elevator ride to the fourth floor were made in a pinched silence. She was grateful Molly was nowhere around to force a conversation of inanities or to see the glisten of tears in her mother's eyes.

The sign of weakness was gone, though, when Merry unlocked the door and turned to take the picnic cloth from Lee. With hardly any effort, he stepped past her and laid the cloth and its contents on the floor beside the dresser.

Merry hesitated in the hallway, her breath fluctuating in her lungs, her palms sweaty with nervousness. What would she do if he tried to kiss her? What would she do if he didn't? Fighting a heart full of emotions she was trying desperately to control, she waited for him to walk past her once more and go out of her life. For good.

Lee did walk past her and her heart jumped to her throat, only to plummet again when he turned and pulled her into his arms. She had no time to resist and no chance to protest before his mouth claimed possession of her lips...maybe he claimed her soul as well. Merry couldn't be sure.

She wasn't even sure she cared. He demanded her response, her absolute attention. There wasn't room in her consciousness for reason or argument. Lee held her and it was the way she'd always dreamed of being held by a man. He kissed her and her heart leaped into his keeping. He touched her breast and she ached to bare it to the massage of his seeking fingers. She wanted to strip off her clothing and his and to lie naked in his arms, to invite him to explore and claim every secret part of her body, every intimate place in her soul. It was madness. And she could no more command it than she could stop her fingertips from curling insistently into his shoulders.

She felt the hard bloom of his desire against her thigh as his tongue plied her lips, teasing, tasting, and finally plunging deeply inside her mouth. Passion seared her skin with a burning fire. She felt hot and cold, and desperately achy. She didn't understand. She'd been kissed—kissed passionately—before. Why was it so different with Lee? How was he able to strip away her veil of composure and leave her exposed and vulnerable to his every whim?

He didn't simply pull away from the embrace, he ended it with cool deliberation. She didn't know how he could be cool. Not when she was so very, very hot. She pressed her hands behind her, hard against the wall, accepting the solid strength, willing her body not to display more weakness. And still the aftermath of the kiss trembled through her like the aftershocks of an earthquake. How could she have lost control? Where was the comfort of anger, outrage, when she so urgently needed it?

"I'll be downstairs in the morning to say goodbye to the Lesters and to Molly." Lee's voice held little inflection or warmth as he made the statement. "It would be rude not to do so. In a few days, maybe a week, I'll be in Austin. I intend to see you then, Merry. You can count on it."

He walked away before she could find the strength to speak. Which was just as well. The only words she could have offered were inappropriate. They were better left unsaid. Lee had disrupted her life, toyed with her emotions, and betrayed her trust for his own purpose. He'd refused to leave her alone. He'd kissed her.

It would be more than foolish to admit now that she was a little bit in love with him.

9

"TRADE SCHEDULES WITH ME!" Janie flopped onto the sofa in the lounge and flung one arm across her forehead. "I can't face Harvey Merton this morning."

"You'd only be trading Harvey's foul temper for Phyllis Gibson's doom and gloom attitude." Merry offered a sympathetic smile. "You wouldn't want to do that, even if Phyllis would let you near her."

"Aaacchh! I'd forgotten about her."

"I thought maybe you had." Merry swallowed the last of the coffee in the Styrofoam cup and tossed it in the wastebasket. "I honestly think I'd rather have a patient scream and cuss at me than to listen to Phyllis catalog a lifetime of insults and injuries."

"She does hold a grudge, doesn't she?"

"Against the whole world."

"Well, she's stayed in therapy with you longer than any other physical therapist." Janie lifted her arm to peep at Merry. "It's probably because she found out you're a 'celebrity' and she hopes you'll mention her in your memoirs."

"Oh, sure," Merry said absently. Her background was hardly a secret among the staff of the Burnstein Clinic, but neither was it a topic for discussion. At the clinic, she was a physical therapist, period. To the other staff members, she was a colleague. To her patients, she was a source of encouragement and a necessary part of the healing process. "It's probably because I'm the only one who doesn't try to cheer her up. I'm convinced she's only happy when she's complaining."

"And what's the fun of complaining if no one will listen, right?" Janie groaned and propped herself up on her elbows. "The rest of us are just envious because you know how to tune her out and still look like you're hanging onto every word."

"Talent, Janie. You know I have loads of it." Merry opened her desk drawer and rummaged through the contents. She withdrew a cellophane-wrapped peppermint candy and slipped it into her pocket. "For Royce," she explained to Janie. "He's first on my schedule today."

"It's hard not to get too attached to a patient like him, isn't it? What a charmer."

"He is that. And he works so hard. Patients like Royce almost make up for the ones like Phyllis."

"And Harvey."

Merry closed the drawer and glanced at the clock. "Almost time. I wouldn't want to keep Royce waiting." She rose and walked toward the doorway. "If he were only a few years older, I might make a play for him myself."

Janie stood and followed Merry to the door. "You always say that about the safe ones, Merry. It's only men like Lee Zurbaron who send you running for cover."

Lee. His name washed over her in waves of memories too fresh to forget. It had been a week and a day and still she couldn't get him out of her mind. Her lips still remembered the taste and the pressure of his. In her dreams, he touched and caressed her in a thousand pleasurable moments. She awakened only to sleep and dream of him again. Nothing she did seemed to make any difference. "You're right, Janie," she answered crisply. "Men like Lee Zurbaron should send any woman running for cover. Any woman with any sense, that is."

"I still think you misjudged him."

"Sure I did." Merry picked up the pace as they proceeded down the hall. She didn't understand why Janie continued to bring up this subject. It wasn't the first time since they'd returned from Galveston, and she hoped it would be the last. "And you don't know the whole story."

"Neither do you, Merry. You wouldn't let him explain."

"He lied. What kind of explanation do you think he'd give, Janie?" Exasperated within the space of a couple of minutes, Merry wondered why she felt this compulsion to defend her stand against Lee. "You need to stop thinking he was such a great guy."

"And you need to stop thinking he's some kind of a . . . a . . . fiend." Janie panted out the last word and, reluctantly, Merry slowed her brisk steps.

"Lee is not a person I can trust, Janie." Merry decided the discussion had gone on long enough. They were almost at the end of the hallway. It was time to put aside personal problems and concentrate on their respective patients. "And that's that."

Janie stopped to catch her breath. "You don't fight fair, Merry. See? My short legs can't keep up with your long ones, not if I have to talk and walk at the same time."

Merry sidestepped her annoyance with Janie and offered a conciliating smile. "You're the one who brought up his name."

"I'm sorry. It's just that—"

Janie looked away and Merry sighed. "What? Spit it out, Janie. Say what you have to say and then we'll close the subject of Lee Zurbaron for good. All right?"

Janie frowned, bit her lower lip, and then looked up at Merry with a steady, serious gaze. "All right, Merry. I'm going to say it straight out. It isn't Lee you can't trust—it's yourself. You're afraid to let any man get too close, whether he knows about your past or not. You avoid men. You worry about what they want from you. You have this crazy idea that if a guy knows about Emerry he couldn't possibly care anything about Merry."

"Ian knew." Merry felt she had to protest, if only to give herself time to think.

Janie brushed at the short blond curls at her temples. "Ian was safe, Merry. I know you genuinely loved him, but I also know there wasn't much passion involved. Not like there is between you and Lee."

"Nonsense. There was nothing but a lie between Lee and me. The only thing he wants is my story. *Emerry's* story."

"Stop worrying about what he wants from you and start thinking about what *you* want. You found something special with that man, Merry. Don't try to deny it, because I won't believe you. You owe it to yourself to find out what it is and what it means to you. It's been years since you took any kind of risk, Merry. It's time."

Hands stuffed in her pockets, Merry turned the cellophane-wrapped candy over and over in her fingers. She hated this type of confrontation and wished Janie didn't try so hard to be such a good friend. There was no way to make her understand.

"I know you mean well, Janie, but I do not need Lee Zurbaron in my life. I have Molly. I have my work. I'm happy. I don't want a man whose interest in me revolves around a career I left behind years ago. It took a long time, but I've finally buried that part of my life and I'm not about to dig it all up again." Merry pushed open the door at the end of the hallway and stepped through into a larger room. "Now, the subject is closed. Agreed?"

Janie stepped through the doorway, frowning whole-heartedly. "Agreed. But—" she pivoted on one foot and faced Merry again "—I still hold to my opinion. You need Lee a heck of a lot more than he needs information for his dissertation. And one other thing, Miss Sunshine, if you've really buried all the crud in your past, then why does it make any difference what Lee, or anyone else, might write about it?"

Janie walked away and Merry was left to deal with the annoying question and a frustrating feeling that she'd been left at the starting gate while Janie, short legs and all, had won the race.

THE FLOWERS ARRIVED at noon. A basketful of gladiolus and baby rosebuds. All colors. Sweet-smelling. A tiny card with a bold message—*See you Friday, Lee.* Merry could feel the determination in the words. *Friday.* In four days.

She wouldn't see him. Tearing the card in half, she tossed it aside and picked up the basket, ready to discard the flowers, too. But she couldn't. The fragrance and sheer beauty of the arrangement stopped her and she set it, again, on the desk. Idly, impulsively, she retrieved the pieces of the card and lay them side by side in front of her. The message remained the same—*See you Friday, Lee*—and after a moment, Merry slipped the torn card into her pocket.

Her fingertips brushed it at least a dozen times that afternoon. And each time, her heart skipped a beat. By Friday morning, she had only to think of the torn card in her pocket and her pulse would race with an anticipation she couldn't control. And she thought of it all too often.

"What are you doing this weekend?" Janie asked as they ate lunch in Merry's office.

"The usual routine. Cleaning, shopping, playing with Molly." But what if Lee actually appeared on her doorstep? Merry wondered. What would she do then? Silly to even think of it. She'd already decided not to see him and she wouldn't waste time wondering about him, either. Resolutely, she sorted through her mail, discarding the junk and separating the rest. When she came across a certified letter, she frowned. "What is she up to now?" Merry said, reaching for the letter opener.

"Who?" Janie asked around a mouthful of apple.

"My mother."

"She's writing to you?"

"I haven't been answering her phone calls, so I guess she . . ." Merry read the letter with a familiar sense of betrayal. "She's been to see her lawyer. The letter's from him."

"Don't tell me. She's going to sue you for not answering your phone."

Merry handed the letter to Janie and rubbed her temples with weary fingers. "She's threatening to sue for visitation rights so she can spend time with her one and only grandchild."

"Why would she do that?"

"To force me to talk to her."

"Seems like a lot of trouble. Maybe she should have written to you herself."

Merry offered a false smile in answer. "That would be too easy, Janie. Emee loves to go the long way around. I know her. You should hear the messages she's been leaving on my answering machine. *'Merry, I don't under-*

stand why you won't talk to me. You know I only want the best for you. Please, call me. I want to talk to Molly. Call me.'"

"Sounds straightforward enough to me."

"You don't know how devious she can be."

"But she's still your mother and Molly's grand-mother. Why not talk to her?" Janie scanned the letter and handed it back. "That'd be a lot better than communicating with her attorney."

Merry sighed and her hand slipped into her pocket. "I'm sure that was her rationale, exactly. She loves to pressure me into doing what she wants by saying I left her no other choice. You just don't understand what it's like not to trust your own mother, Janie. It isn't pleasant, I can tell you."

Janie crunched the last bite of her apple in a thoughtful silence. "Well, what are you going to do?"

"I suppose I'll call an attorney and find out how far she can legally go with her demands and then . . . I don't know. Maybe she'll undergo a miraculous change of heart and become a genuine person. The kind of mother I've always wanted."

Janie stood up, gathered the leftovers of her lunch, and moved to the door. "And maybe you'll turn into the daughter she always wanted. It sounds to me as if both of you need a crash course in acceptance. You know, my mother and I don't agree on everything either." Janie chuckled suddenly, as if the mere thought of that was ridiculous. "In fact, I think the only thing we're in complete accord about is that Ken is a terrific guy."

"And she adores your girls," Merry pointed out.

"True, but she doesn't adore my mothering skills. How she loves to tell me I'm ruining them . . . then she turns right around and spoils them rotten." Janie shook her head. "See, Merry, your mother isn't so different. She just wants a chance to spoil Molly without your supervision."

"I don't think that's it, Janie."

"Maybe not." One round shoulder lifted in a shrug as Janie opened the door and waved goodbye. "If you and Molly want to come for potluck tonight, you're both welcome. Ken has to work, so it'll just be me and the girls. See ya."

Merry drank the last of her fruit juice and regarded the letter from Emee's attorney with a critical eye. Acceptance, Janie had said. But she didn't know Emee. There was more to this tangled mother/daughter relationship than an inability to accept the other person. No matter how much Emee tried to sound like a wounded parent, no matter how many times sincerity rang in her words, Merry didn't trust her. How could she?

So, with hardly any hesitation, Merry called an attorney and made an appointment to see him the next week. The idea that her own mother was pushing her to the limit rankled though, and throughout the afternoon it irritated her more and more. Almost as much as the way she jumped every time someone entered the therapy room, the way her breath caught every time she heard voices out in the hallway. Her hand stayed in her jacket pocket, touching Lee's card, telling herself he wouldn't come and that, even if he did, she wouldn't see him.

By the time she finished the last therapy session of the day, she felt raw and ready to scream at the slightest provocation. Maybe she would call Emee, she thought. Maybe she'd let her know how little she appreciated these attempts to manipulate her and Molly's lives. Maybe she'd call Lee, too. Tell him not to send flowers with cryptic notes that meant nothing. Nothing.

She lingered in her office just to avoid the cheery goodnights of her co-workers and to try to regain a measure of composure before picking up Molly. The thought of her daughter's happy smile gave Merry the boost she needed and she straightened Molly's picture on her desk before leaving the clinic.

As she stepped outside, she shaded her eyes against the afternoon sun and searched her purse for her sunglasses. As she placed them on the bridge of her nose, she started for her car.

"Good-looking glasses."

The voice stopped her feet and her heart all in the same instant. *Lee.* She spun toward the sound. He stood not two feet away from her, dressed in blue jeans and a polo shirt, a pair of dark glasses set squarely on his face, shielding her from the intensity of his gaze, keeping her from seeing any emotion written there.

How had she not seen him the moment she left the building? How had she failed to sense his presence so close by? Her body fairly shook with sensations now and she couldn't seem to look anywhere except at him. Tall, tanned, he was the image in a thousand memories she hadn't been able to forget. Sensual, seductive, he was the dream lover she couldn't escape in the night. Her first instinct was to walk straight into his arms and let reason go to hell.

"What are you doing here?" she said instead.

"Waiting for you."

"Why?"

A muscle in his jaw tensed—relaxed. "Because I had to see you again. I've missed you, Merry."

She wanted to believe him so badly her fingernails bit into the soft skin of her palm. "You and my mother, Lee," she said with exquisite composure. "You both miss what I can do for you."

"Really?" His voice dropped to a pleasant baritone, picking up a hint of irritation on the way. "And what is it you can do for me, Merry?"

"Help with your precious book. But you know I won't, so you try a different tactic, a roundabout way of getting the information you need. You pretend your interest in me is a personal one."

He regarded her in silence for a moment. He would walk away, now, she thought. He would go out of her life and leave her in peace. She waited, her breath suspended in her throat.

"Janie told me you'd had a rough day." The soft statement reflected neither anger nor any intention of walking out of her life. "It sounds as if she was right."

Merry searched her brain for some other way to discourage him. Or maybe she only wanted to discourage her own wayward impulses. "Janie shouldn't have said anything to you."

He took a step forward. "Luckily, she didn't feel that way. She was very pleasant."

"She's very shortsighted."

"I see you haven't changed your opinion of me in the past week."

"A year, ten years won't make any difference, Lee. But maybe you'll find comfort in the idea that you were one of the bigger disappointments in my life."

"Tell me about the disappointments, Merry. I'm a good listener."

"How well I know." The day's frustrations, the week's uncertainties suddenly flooded her with anger. She pulled off the sunglasses and faced him, furious and yet trembling like a frightened child inside. "You'll listen and then tell the world. I've met men like you before."

"I don't think so. I'm one of a kind."

Merry shook her head, indicating in a single motion that he was of the dime-a-dozen variety. But her heart knew he was right. Lee *was* different. And that's why his deception hurt so much. "I guess I must ask you one more time to leave me alone, Lee."

The lines of his mouth tightened as he reached up and removed his glasses. He blinked against the sunlight, but his dark eyes never wavered from hers. "I can't do that, Merry. The truth is, you won't leave *me* alone. For a week now, I've walked the beach in Galveston trying to get a little perspective on my feelings for you. Everywhere I looked, I saw you. At night, I dreamed about you. During the day, I went over our conversations, word by word. I can't get you out of my mind. It's not as if I can control this, Merry. Anymore than you can."

The words rang with an irrefutable truth. He was right. She hadn't been in control since that afternoon on the plane. But she would get it back. She had to. Even if it meant denying her own feelings. "I can control it, Lee, and I will. Go back to California. Counsel people with real problems. Write a book about them. I don't care what you do as long as it doesn't involve me."

She turned to leave, but he reached for her, his fingers closing insistently over her forearm. "You care, Merry. No matter how many times you tell yourself you don't."

His touch stole her breath away and robbed her of the anger she needed in order to convince him he was wrong. She didn't care. He was wrong. Wrong. And yet, his hand on her arm, his warmth against her skin, belied her conviction. Doubt wavered beneath an onslaught of emotions. She seized a stronger hold on her waning control and summoned the courage to dismiss him once and for all. But the final words refused to leave her lips and in their place she heard a faint moan of surrender. "What do you want from me, Lee? What in sweet heaven do you want?"

"Time, Merry. Give me, give us, a chance to discover each other. Talk to me. Give me time to prove myself. Let me be your friend. Let me know you. Let me help you come to terms with your feelings."

Sincerity rang in his voice and was echoed in the clear gaze he kept on her. The intensity of his emotion flowed from his fingertips into her arm and followed the trail of warmth his touch had sent through her body only moments before. She wanted to believe him, but the only words that lingered in her mind were ones he hadn't actually said. *I only want what's best for you.* Emee's words, but inherent, also, in his plea for understanding. The anger returned as suddenly as it had left and she shook herself free of his hold.

"Oh, come on, Lee. Be honest enough to admit you want my help so you can finish your precious book." She turned from him and walked toward her car. "Call Emee. She's dying to tell you anything and everything you want to know. Collaborate with her and leave me out of it."

"For the last time, Merry, this is my dissertation, the final step in obtaining my doctorate. Why do you insist upon referring to it as a book?" He stepped in between her and the car, blocking her retreat, forcing her to face him.

"There's more money to be made from a book, Lee. Don't tell me you haven't thought of that."

"Thought of what? Writing a book? Yes, as a matter of fact, I have." He crossed his arms and leaned against her car. "But at the moment, I'm only interested in completing my degree and trying—God knows why—to get you to listen to me."

"So you can tell me how wrong I am? No, thank you. My mother does a magnificent job doing that all by herself." She reached for the car door handle, but made contact with a lean, muscled thigh, instead. She withdrew her hand, but her eyes sought his in sudden awareness. "I have to pick up Molly. I'm late, now."

"I'll go with you. I'll take you both out to dinner."

"No." She gave the word as much emphasis as the long day and her depleted resources would allow. In truth, she would have liked to lay her head on his shoulder and tell him all her fears, about him, about her mother's threatening letter, about life in general. What a mistake that would be. She lifted her gaze. "Go away, Lee. Just go away."

"Not until you've heard me out." His expression changed, his voice soft with persuasion. "Why are you afraid of talking to me, Merry? Not about my dissertation. Not about Emerry. About you. I only want to talk about you."

Oh, he was good. Even better than Emee at manipulating emotion. She could see through him, though. She knew that the bottom line would come down to Emerry and Emerry's reasons for leaving fame and fortune behind. She knew it. And despite the warnings of hard-won logic, she knew she was going to agree. Maybe because it had been a frustrating day. Maybe because he, of all the men she'd ever met, had touched her heart. He'd been a hero . . . if only for a moment. And she wanted him to realize the consequences of his betrayal.

"You want to talk, Lee?" She asked in a cynical tone, as she placed the sunglasses back on her nose. "All right.

I'll give you time to talk. But I give you fair warning that I'm out of patience with people who try to manipulate me."

"That's all right. I mean, I understand." He was so surprised by her agreement he almost laughed aloud. She'd offered him another chance. If he couldn't convince her his intentions were honorable and sincere, he wasn't as much in love with her as he'd decided he must be. "Shall I drive? Or will you? I could follow you or—"

"I have to take care of Molly first. You can come to my house at seven-thirty." She gave him the address in a cool tone. But despite her indifference, he repeated it twice, memorizing the address and smiling at her.

"I'll bring something for dinner," he said.

"No dinner, Lee. This is not a social engagement. You want to talk. I've agreed. There is nothing more to it than that."

There was plenty more to it. The slightest blush on her cheek betrayed her. Her hand quivered as she pushed the key in the lock and opened the car door. Her movements lacked their usual finesse.

He made her nervous.

No, he made her tremble. The knowledge awed him and left him shaky. No woman had ever made him feel so confident and yet so unsure of himself. But then, no woman had ever mattered as much.

"Seven-thirty," he said and held the door as she slid onto the seat.

She didn't say goodbye, just started the car and drove away. He wondered if he'd pushed her too hard, applied too much pressure, and knew even as the question was posed in his mind, that he had done just that. But Merry didn't give any quarter. She closed her heart and her mind to the mere threat of an intruder. On the plane, in Galveston, he'd gotten a glimpse of what she hid behind that veil of composure...and he couldn't forget. He was lost . . . and wasn't sure he'd ever find himself again. Not if he had to do it away from her. Gut instinct told him she was worth the small sacrifice of propriety. His heart told him she was worth any and every effort required.

Emerry, be damned, he thought. Merry was all, and more, than he'd hoped to find. If only she would listen . . .

10

IT WAS A MISTAKE.

She knew it when she drove out of the clinic's parking lot and glanced in the rearview mirror. Lee was watching her and, despite the distance, despite the shading of dark glasses, she recognized his elation. He was happy with her concession, pleased to have another shot at cracking her silence. Why had she exposed herself to that? What self-destructive mechanism kicked in whenever he got within ten feet of her?

Picking up Molly at the sitter's, Merry found a moment of respite from self-incrimination. She called Janie and arranged for Molly to stay overnight. She gently refused a second offer of potluck with the girls, pleading a headache and a dozen chores. If Janie noticed anything amiss, she didn't comment on it. A lapse for which Merry was deeply grateful. By the time she'd returned home, showered, and changed into a cool knit top and sarong skirt, she was ready to face Lee. She'd show him how effectively she could control this situation.

"Hi," he said when she opened the door in answer to his knock. He stood, empty-handed, in her doorway. She'd expected he would bring something...flowers, wine, a gift. It was the type of gesture most men would have made, a concession to her reluctance to see him, an offering to appease any lingering anger. She'd been so sure he would try to win a measure of approval that way, she'd practiced saying a nonchalant thank-you. And now, she didn't quite know what to say.

"Come in." She stepped back, allowing him to come in. Her hand pressed so hard against the edge of the door, she felt its imprint on her palm. Okay, she thought, as she gently massaged the marks, she was a little nervous. But in control. Definitely, in control.

"Is Molly here?" he asked.

"No." She motioned him to precede her into the living room and followed at a safe distance.

"This isn't the way I pictured your house." Lee wandered to the flowered-chintz sofa and ran a fingertip along its curved arm. "I thought it would be..." His gaze roamed the walls, paused to note the baskets and straw fans, continued on to the bookshelves, the fireplace, the few knickknacks scattered here and there, and went on to search for signs of something Merry couldn't identify.

His unfinished comment unsettled her, made the first dent in her studied composure. What was missing? What did he see, or not see, that surprised him? What did this room, this house, reflect of her that he saw immediately upon entering? "I decorated it myself," she said because it seemed necessary to defend her choices.

A smile tipped his mouth, drawing her gaze to the curve of his lips. "Yes, I can see that. It's lovely, Merry. This room is very warm, very comfortable. I like it. Is this where you want to talk?"

Just like that, he gained the upper hand. He walked into her home and, somehow, took possession of it. He cut the small talk and set the parameters of their confrontation concisely and without hesitation. He looked at her and she felt weak. Control began to slip and she made a desperate grab for it. "This is fine." Her voice sounded as tight as a violin string. It felt even tighter. She swallowed and her hand made an expansive sweep toward the sofa. "Make yourself comfortable."

He glanced at the seat she indicated, but remained standing. His smile was confident, sure, and yet oddly vulnerable. "If you're going to stand, I think I'll do that, too."

She moved to a chair and sat on the edge of an overly plump cushion. "Okay," she said and was relieved when he sank onto the sofa. Her breath came in shallow spurts, a result, perhaps, of her fluctuating heartbeat. It couldn't be that Lee's presence in her living room unnerved her. No. She wasn't so foolish as to be taken in by the way he smiled. Or the relaxed way he fit into his surroundings.

She wasn't relaxed. Her back wasn't anywhere near the chair, her spine was ramrod straight. She'd never felt so uncomfortable in her own home. How did he do this? Why did she let him?

"All right, Lee." She crossed her arms at her waist and challenged him with her eyes. "Say whatever it is you have to say."

He leaned forward, hands loosely clasped, eyes fixed on her face. "I think I'm in love with you, Merry."

She shot up from her seat and then, realizing her legs wouldn't support her for long, she sank back to the cushion. This was crazy. Crazy. She raked a hand through the long strands of her hair, realized how much agitation the gesture displayed and tucked the hand safely in her lap. "In a pig's eye," she said crisply.

He blinked, but his smile, of all things, returned in full force. "I don't have much experience in this kind of situation, but 'in a pig's eye' wasn't quite the response I'd hoped for."

"Oh, really? Did you think I'd swoon with delight and shyly confess that I'm in love with you, too?"

"You are?"

"No!" She stood again, taking a couple of steps away from the safety of the chair. She needed to be on her feet for this. "No. Do you think I'm so naive I'd fall for such a typical ploy? Men have been professing their love for me since I was old enough to wear lip gloss. I got letters proposing marriage when I was barely thirteen. By sixteen, I'd been propositioned more times than I could remember. Don't try to pull this stunt with me, Lee. You're no more in love than . . . than. . . ." Words failed her and she turned away from his steady gaze.

"You don't believe me." His voice was calm, soothing, filled with an acceptance of her right to doubt him. He stood up, too. She was aware of that and stiffened against any approach he might make. But he didn't take a single step toward her . . . or away from her. "Why don't you believe me?"

She spun on her heel, angry—or perhaps afraid—that he could see past her outburst to the raw emotion just below the surface. "Well, I'll tell you." She paused to discipline her voice and to clasp her hands so they wouldn't tremble. "I know from personal experience how far some people will go to get what they want. You want information, Lee, and you've just proven you'll say anything to get it."

"Is that what I did?"

"I'm an expert at reading between the lines, Lee. My mother taught me. She's mastered the art of saying one thing and meaning something entirely different. Why just today she—" No, she wouldn't tell him that. For all she knew, Emee could have sent him . . . a sort of followup on her letter. Was it coincidence that brought Lee to her on the same day? Merry couldn't afford to deny the possibility.

Lee waited a while before he spoke. Merry's anger distressed him. He wanted to comfort her, hold her, defend her against Emee...or the whole world if necessary. She wouldn't allow that, he knew. His only option was to get her to open up. "Just today what?" he asked softly. "What did your mother do today, Merry?"

"Nothing. I haven't spoken with her in days."

"So why are you upset?"

Merry had no intention of telling him. It was none of his business. But when she opened her mouth to inform him of that, she found herself confiding in him despite her intentions. Lee just seemed to have that effect on her. "She had her attorney write a letter to suggest that I should set up a schedule of visitation between grandmother and granddaughter. It seems Emee wishes to spend more time *alone* with Molly. She wants Molly to be allowed to visit her in Denver...or wherever she may be. The threat of further legal action wasn't mentioned, but it was implied. As I told you, I've learned to read between the lines."

"Do you object to her seeing Molly?"

"I object to her plans for Molly's future. I don't want her to use Molly the way she used me, the way she uses everyone. Even you, Lee. She didn't tell you how to find me out of altruism. She pointed you in the right direction because she knew it was the perfect way to manipulate me into doing what she wants. You're doing research on child stars. If you can persuade me to help you, then I'll have to remember how wonderful it was to be Little Miss Sunshine. And then...well, in Emee's mind, I'll realize that Molly was born to follow in my footsteps. Emee would love that. It would give her another chance to 'shine'."

Merry drew a deep breath, folded her arms beneath her breast, released them again. "It's all the same to her, you see. Emee loves the spotlight. She should have been the model, but she didn't have the opportunities. So she made sure that I did."

"She lived vicariously through you," Lee commented and Merry nodded.

"The glamour of my career was all she ever dreamed it would be. She loved everything about those years. She loved the money, the famous people, the jet set life-style, the whole glittering facade. It didn't matter that I didn't share that love, that I was shy and hated the spotlight. Because *she* wanted it, we lived it. And she'd make the choices for Molly, too, if I allowed it." Merry regretted the flow of words, regretted showing the part of her those words revealed. She felt disloyal to her mother, though she owed Emee no loyalty, and she felt a sense of disloyalty to herself, as well. This was the kind of information Lee wanted about her past, and she'd handed it to him on a silver platter. Even after she'd promised herself she wouldn't tell him anything. The anger she'd nurtured all evening turned inward.

"Well, there you have it, Lee. Some of the juicy background on Emerry Emilia Edwards and her pushy mother." Merry scooped back the weight of hair falling forward at her temples and frowned at Lee.

He said nothing, but there was understanding in his eyes, concern in the set of his jaw. His undemanding silence highlighted Merry's lack of composure and she wanted to say something, anything, to jar him and force him to stop acting as if he really cared about her. "Isn't that what you came here for? Some insight into Emerry, the child star, the luckiest little girl in the world? Maybe you should write it down. Or maybe you brought a tape recorder. That would be better, wouldn't it? Then you could quote me verbatim, right?"

Still, he gave no answer and a swirl of panic swept over her. She was telling him things she'd never told anyone and he just stood there. Why didn't he say something? "What is it, Lee? Didn't I give you enough information? Do you want more? There's never enough, is there? Not for people like you and Emee."

He moved, then. Quickly and quietly, with compelling determination, he came close to her and placed his hands on her shoulders, turning her to face him and tilting her chin with a firm knuckle. "I came here to tell you that I'm falling in love with you, Merry. I want very much to write about your experiences in my dissertation, but that has nothing to do with the way I feel about you. I'm not Emee. There's nothing to read between the lines, no ulterior motives."

His expression was honest, his voice sincere, and she wanted desperately to believe what he said. When she raised her eyes and sought to find the truth in his, she felt the whisper of his breath on her lips, the pressure of his hands on her back. For a moment, there was a pulsing silence, an acute awareness of how very close together they stood. Then he drew her—or perhaps she went of her own accord—into his arms and her lips parted in full acceptance of his kiss.

As their mouths fused in a hungry coupling, Merry lost the last remnant of self-control . . . if she'd possessed it to begin with. Lee made her forget everything. He opened up his arms and she walked into the trap like a butterfly caught in a spider's web. All her efforts to distance herself from him only seemed to bring her closer to her fate. And if this . . . this heady, intoxicating feeling . . . was fate, then she could no longer fight it.

Her body swayed against his, molding and sculpting her curves into his angles, binding her weakness to his strength. Her skirt rode up on her thigh, and her skin rubbed against the rough denim covering his legs. Her hands slipped around him and she felt the corded muscles of his shoulders and lower back. Sensations ran rampant from her fingertips and up the length of her arms to race in a frenzy of impulses throughout her body. Her breasts ached to be touched, kissed, and caressed and she felt the nipples grow hard with the thought.

It was a betrayal she hadn't expected. She had every reason to doubt Lee's motives, every reason to believe he would do anything to gain the information he wanted. And once he had it, she would mean nothing to him. Emerry would be the only one who mattered.

It was sobering to realize she didn't care. Not when he kissed her this way. Not when his musky male scent filled her nostrils. Not when his tongue mated sensuously, seductively with hers. All that mattered was his touch and her need for more of it.

His hands moved to cup her hips, to pull her closer to her fate and from some frightened corner of her heart, Merry managed to find a scrap of resistance. She had to protest. She couldn't just let him.

He lifted his head, leaving her lips warm and swollen with his passion. His dark eyes—almost black in the intensity of the moment—locked with hers and she knew it was now or never. In another second, when he claimed her kiss again, it would be forever too late. "I—" The whisper barely registered as a sigh, so soft, so tentative. She tried again. "I don't trust you, Lee. I don't—"

"Oh, yes, you do, Merry," he corrected her with a voice as soft as hers, but not at all uncertain. "You trust me more than you're willing to admit. And I'm going to prove it to you right now."

Tenderly, purposefully, he took possession of her. Not just her lips, but her breath, her heartbeat, her . . . heart. Where he touched her, she burned. Her skin radiated heat, *his* heat and her own. A slow fever wrapped around and around her. Fires sparked through her body like matches to seasoned kindling. She wanted this man, wanted him so badly she was willing to forsake all reason in order to have him. If only for one night. If only for one hour. He had created an ache inside her that wouldn't be satisfied. He'd betrayed her and yet, if going to bed with him would exorcise the gnawing hunger inside her, then it was a small price to pay. Maybe not a price at all, but a ransom. Sex in exchange for peace of mind.

But it wasn't simply sex. Sex was something that happened for a lot of reasons between a man and a woman. She'd experienced it, knew its illusory promise rarely came to fruition. At worst, it was unsatisfying. At best, a physical release of tension. Sometimes she'd found a warm contentment that lingered for awhile.

But this was hunger, a raw, poignant need to be joined with Lee, bonded to him in body and spirit. She felt hot in places she hadn't known could feel that way. Contentment seemed as far from her grasp as the moon. Her heart pounded furiously as if ready to wing its way from her body. Her breath stopped, started, stopped again with every movement he made. Whatever chemistry existed for her with Lee, Merry recognized its power and knew it was far beyond her ability to keep in check. Passion seemed too tame a word to describe it. She *desired* Lee, and the feeling was terrifying, new and exciting. Very exciting.

She admitted it freely, though silently, when his hand found the single button that held her sarong skirt in place. It crumpled to the floor and folded at her feet. She never wore slips and it was too hot for hosiery, so beneath the skirt she was bare-legged and covered only by a strip of silk and lace not much wider than the palms of Lee's hands.

Had she dressed so provocatively intentionally? Had her subconscious obeyed a secret impulse to wear something easily discarded and intimately seductive? She didn't want to think she could be so . . . so provocative. But whether or not she'd dressed for seduction, the effect was the same. She heard the quick intake of his breath, felt the tension snap taut in the stillness, and knew that what he saw pleased him. Yet in the back of her mind, she understood that had her legs been shorter, fuller, not slim and long, had her body been less sleek, less sensual, still he would have been pleased. It wasn't her body alone he intended to possess, but her soul as well.

The knowledge nestled deep in her heart and took root there. Maybe he'd been honest. Maybe, just maybe, he was a little bit in love with her.

His hands curved at her waist, thumbs resting against her ribs, fingers splayed at her back. Slowly, he pushed up the hem of her knit blouse, grazing her skin with a fingertip caress, easing the material upward. She held her breath as he reached her breasts and pulled the fabric smoothly away, then up and over her head, bringing her arms up and out in graceful synchronization.

He looked at her for endless seconds before he moved to lift her into his arms. Merry made no protest at his possessive manner as he carried her to the sofa and laid her down. He stroked her face, soothing the wayward strands of hair, touching her lips with his palms, then with his fingertips and then, sweetly, with his mouth. "When will Molly be home?" he asked, allowing only the narrowest of space between his lips and hers.

"Tomorrow." She was breathless and it was all she could do to whisper the word.

Again, his fingertip brushed the corners of her mouth with tender purpose. "May I stay with you tonight?"

Did he think she had the willpower to refuse? She nodded her consent and felt a thrill of pleasure that he'd asked. Now. Not later. He would be with her all night. After the lovemaking, he would hold her, sleep next to her. It was, she thought, a comforting thing to know...now. Later, she would deal with the consequences and her feelings. Tomorrow, perhaps. For the moment, she could only respond...and enjoy.

With a roving finger, he traced a line from her chin over her throat and down to the hollow in her shoulder. There, he placed a kiss. His tongue took up the exploration and made a moist, warm journey along the curve of her neck, lingering, teasing and finally reaching the swell of her breast.

Merry lay still, dying a little with every moment it took for him to push aside the lacy cup of her bra and tantalize her waiting nipple with wet, circling strokes of his tongue. When she raised her hands to the buttons of his shirt, he pulled up to give her room. She was nervous, though, and the buttons stayed in place, so after a moment, Lee stood up and removed his clothes. All of them.

She'd seen him in a swimsuit, knew the muscled expanse of his torso and the strong, tanned length of his legs. But naked and revealed in a stage of obvious arousal, he fascinated her. Her gaze traveled across the golden-brown hair on his abdomen and chest and reached his eyes. She saw her own intimate longings reflected there and, with a sudden shyness, she let her gaze move downward again.

Lee noticed the slow blush move into her cheeks and was touched by it. He knelt beside the sofa and rubbed the back of his hand against her skin, letting his fingers trail along her arm to her shoulder, across the hollows of her neck, up over her chin to rest on her slightly parted lips. His body throbbed with the need to cover hers. His heart pounded so hard he thought she surely must hear it. A faint moisture broke across his back, a sign of the restraint he exercised on his desire.

He would not rush. Not by a touch, not by a whispered word of passion. These moments were too special, too important. He'd prove to Merry how much he cared for her. He'd love her so tenderly that her heart could have no doubt about his sincerity.

Easing the straps of her bra over her shoulders revealed a new and alluring view of soft breasts rising and falling beneath his gaze. With sure, unhurried movements he lifted her and unsnapped the hook, pulling away the lingerie and tossing it aside. He cupped her breasts in his hands and lowered his head to place a kiss on each pebble hard peak before turning his attention to delights lower down.

Merry shivered as he traced a moist trail of desire along her stomach, to the top of her thigh. He removed her panties, sliding the silky strip one torturously slow inch at a time, heating her skin with the zephyr-soft brush of his fingertips. Finally, when she lay naked before him, he smiled and with gentleness that tore at her heart, he slipped off her shoes. First one, then the other. Then beginning with her feet, he explored her body with his gaze, his fingers, his lips.

And with every touch, with each new secret pleasure he discovered, Merry melted deeper into a world of fiery sensations. Her blood pumped through her veins with the urgency of a river in a torrential flood. She sought to hold him against her, but her hands were restless, her arms lacked the strength to keep him in one place. When the need became too great, the pleasures too intense, she called to him and he moved over her like a warm, rushing tide. Her arms encircled his waist, her hands investigated the planes of his back, the slope of his powerful hips, the rough texture of his thighs. She slipped a hand between their bodies and found him, hard and pulsating. Firmly, gently, she guided him toward a mutual fulfillment.

When he stopped and lifted himself away, she felt bereft and achingly needy. But as she realized he was taking a moment to protect her, a sense of warmth spooled through her and banished any thought of abandonment. He came back to her with a tender smile. Merry caught her breath and reached for him again.

Once joined with her, he slowed the pace and took long, seductive drinks of her lips. His tongue flirted with hers, dancing, tasting, until she responded without hesitation and opened her mouth wide to his invasion. Every hungering, secret place in her body accepted and delighted in his touch. Every hungering, lonely place in her heart reached out for the promise of his love. She could neither stop the flow of emotions nor the spasms of sheer delight that gripped her.

When the glorious sensations peaked and washed through her in widening ripples of ecstasy, she gasped, clinging to Lee with body and soul, loving him totally in that instant of exquisite oblivion. He shuddered against her, whispering sweet satisfaction, and holding her tight as they were swept into the current of a wild and raging sea.

Through a sated fog of serenity, Merry became aware of Lee's weight bearing gently down on her body. It made her feel warm and fragile and feminine. His breath peppered her skin with uneven warmth. One hand rested loosely on her breast. His fingers toyed with a strand of her hair. She luxuriated in the lazy touches. How nice it felt to be close to him. How good it was to be held and touched and loved.

She brought up her hand and stroked the back of his head until he raised himself and looked into her eyes. "That was beautiful, Merry-as-in-Christmas. So beautiful."

"Yes," she whispered, allowing herself to drown for a moment in his warm, dark eyes. It would be foolish and futile to deny the beauty of the moments they'd just shared. Just as it would be foolish and futile to believe it could last. But for now, for a few hours, she wouldn't think about that. She would think only about the sweet satisfaction he had brought to her and the tender promise his body had offered—might offer again.

"I'm staying with you tonight," he reminded her as if he thought she might send him away.

A sigh parted her lips and Lee accepted the quiet invitation. As his mouth closed tenderly over hers, Merry wondered if it was his or her own wanton desires she couldn't deny. Deep in her heart, she knew she shouldn't let him stay, she shouldn't let him touch her...there...or there. But she had neither the will nor the wish to stop him. She had surrendered her control and she wasn't sure how she was going to get it back.

But as Lee's kiss deepened, drawing her response, culling a honeyed pleasure from her lips, renewing a heated yearning deep inside her, she couldn't think why it would matter.

11

MERRY AWAKENED ALONE and immediately missed Lee. The covers were pushed back on his side of the bed, but the sheets were rumpled and when she ran her hand across them, she caught the faint scent of his cologne. She closed her eyes and let the memory of last night's love-making play through her thoughts.

It was all there—the breathtaking ecstasy of his touch, the tender way he'd held her tight against his hard body, the satisfied sigh he'd expelled when they settled to-gether on her bed. They'd talked, drifted into a con-tented silence, and then made love again. Lee had kept their lovers' conversation on the light side, telling her bits and pieces of his life, anecdotes that made her smile and taught her small, but important lessons about him. She had asked the hundred and one questions she'd failed to ask before and wondered why she'd been so afraid to really know him. Had she really thought she could pro-tect herself from involvement by hiding behind a veil of indifference?

Lying beside him, filled with the sensations he evoked in her, sated with his lovemaking and yet hungry for more, she'd known she was involved. Far out of her depth. Her uninhibited passion gave proof to that . . . if she'd needed any.

Merry had hardly recognized the person she'd be-come in Lee's arms. Her body burned with a seemingly insatiable fever, her mind refused to consider the consequences of her actions. For the hours of the night, she was a stranger to herself . . . a woman held fast in the throes of love.

But now it was morning. She was alone. Her seducer was no longer near enough to steal her sanity with his kisses or to melt her doubts with a touch. And the doubts were there. Muted, but still present in the back of her mind.

She rolled onto her side, hugging the pillow, and wondered where Lee had gone. Beyond the bedroom door, she could hear the rustle of movement and knew he hadn't left the house. A slow smile eased onto her lips in the same way a lazy contentment drifted around her. It had been a long time since she'd experienced the pleasure of waking up and knowing a man—her man—was close by.

Hers? The word echoed in her head and her heart. No, that couldn't be. Why, she hardly knew Lee. She certainly had no claim on him. In fact, when she had time to think, she would probably be totally disgusted about allowing a physical passion to overcome her better judgment. At the moment, it was hard to imagine how she could ever feel disgusted about such a beautiful experience, but . . .

She rolled from her side to her back and stared at the ceiling. Something was cooking, now. The aroma wended its way from the kitchen into the bedroom and her stomach stirred slightly at the tantalizing smell. Lee was making breakfast, she thought. A strange man was looking through her cabinets, helping himself to her groceries, learning where she kept the utensils, the plates, the seasonings.

Was that so terrible? Why did she worry about what he might find, what he might see, what he might know about her? After last night, her distrust of Lee was foolish. He'd proven her wrong...one sensual time after another. She did trust him. She must. Otherwise, she wouldn't be lying in bed, hoping for his return, while he made breakfast in her kitchen.

She glanced over to see him hesitating in the doorway. "Hi," he said and her heart squeezed tight with the tenderness of his smile. "Want something to eat?"

She didn't. With his presence filling her room, her thoughts turned to other physical needs and she felt the heat wander through her veins. Slowly, she shook her head. Her gaze traveled over him, eager to see and memorize his morning appearance. From attractively disheveled hair to a shadow of a beard, from bare feet to the top two open buttons on his shirt, she loved the way he looked. If she'd had an ounce less restraint, she'd have lured him back into bed then and there.

"You're up early," she said instead and cleared her voice of a curious huskiness.

"I knew if I stayed in bed, I'd wake you. And I thought you needed your sleep. You didn't get much last night." He grinned gently. "Much *sleep*, I mean."

The heat stopped its wandering and centered in her cheeks. She never blushed. It had been one of the reasons she'd been a good model. But under her lover's gaze, lying naked between the sheets, aware of the intimacy they had shared, she blushed. "What's cooking?" She strove for a nonchalant tone and knew by his deepening smile that she had failed.

"Overcooked eggs and blackened biscuits?" she suggested mischievously.

He stood still for a while before he advanced on the bed. "You got it, lady," he growled seductively as he reached for the button closure of his jeans. A few seconds later he'd shucked his clothes and was on the bed beside her, his hands roaming her body teasingly.

Lee loved her with a fierce and gentle passion. Their hunger was no less intense than the night before, and it held the sweet promise of fulfillment experienced by new lovers. It confirmed Merry's realization that, somehow, without her knowledge or consent, her heart had made a commitment to Lee. Although it didn't make sense she couldn't deny it—any more than she could deny her body's eager response....

THE SMOKE ALARM went off just as the odor of burning bread filtered into the bedroom and Lee laughed at the appropriate timing. "Either we're hot lovers or your blackened biscuits are done," he said as he pressed a fleeting kiss to her lips and bounded out of bed to handle the crisis.

Merry lay for a few minutes, feeling too lazily content to move. It was lucky the biscuits had lasted as long as they had, she thought. If the alarm had sounded a few minutes sooner, she wasn't sure what would have happened. It would certainly have interrupted an idyllic moment. On the other hand, it might have gone unheeded and the kitchen would have caught on fire. She smiled languidly and then tossed back the covers, reached for a robe, and followed Lee to the kitchen.

"You're pretty good at this." She fanned smoke with her hand. "Do you use this recipe often?"

He climbed down from the chair he'd stood on to shut off the alarm, totally at ease with being naked in her kitchen. "This is my first attempt and, if I do say so myself, I think it was highly successful." He dropped a pat on her bottom and moved past her to take a tray of dark—very dark—biscuits from the oven. "All depends on how hungry you are."

Merry tore her gaze from the intriguing view of his tight buttocks and eyed the burnt crusts skeptically. She wrinkled her nose at the sight of two rubbery-looking eggs. "Maybe we should go out for breakfast."

"Good idea. What about Molly?"

"I don't think she'd like these biscuits, either."

"In that case, we'll pick her up on our way to the restaurant." Lee slipped an oven mitt over his hand and lifted the tray. "You don't mind, do you?"

"No. Molly will love it," Merry said absently, her thoughts lingering on the hard length of his body and the sexy tan marks. "She loves eating out."

"I meant about the biscuits. It was the last mix you had."

"The last one?" Merry said in mock dismay. "You burned the *last* biscuit mix I had?"

"Well, you did offer some assistance. If you hadn't distracted me, I wouldn't have let them stay in the oven so long."

"Are you insinuating that I made you do it?"

His eyes darkened as he responded to her teasing with a caressing gaze over her scantily clad body. "Yes, Merry, I am insinuating just that. And if you want to press the issue, we can forget about breakfast." A smile tucked in at the corner of his mouth. "We'll go out for lunch instead. I burn a mean grilled cheese sandwich."

She was tempted. Oh, she was tempted. "I can't have you setting off the smoke alarm all day, Lee. I have errands to run and housework to do."

"I'll help. Then we'll take Molly to the park."

Merry frowned, forcing her gaze to match up with his and not settle on other distracting perspectives of his naked body. "I can't, really."

"Of course, you can." He found the trash container under the sink and dumped the burned biscuits. "I'll help you with everything you need to do. I'm a good house-keeper."

Merry felt the first chink in her contented morning. "Look, Lee. You don't have to spend the day here. Last night was . . . well, it happened. I didn't intend for us to . . . get involved and I'm not sure I know how I feel about it or about you."

"Do you think I planned what happened?" he asked in a suddenly serious tone.

"I don't know." She paused to consider his question. "I think it's possible that you did. You have to understand, Lee, that I have no reason to believe you and a good reason not to. You want something from me. This could be your way of getting it." She regretted the accusation immediately, but couldn't make herself apologize for voicing the doubt. He'd deceived her once. And as much as she hated to admit it, she was aware that he had the power to do so again. She'd never been so vulnerable.

His expression hardened with her statement and he turned his back to her. He scraped the overcooked eggs into the disposal and washed out the skillet. His movements were stilted and jerky, as if he had to exercise enormous control to avoid confronting her with his anger. After a couple of minutes, he seemed to relax and walked over to her. He placed his hands, still a bit moist from the water, on her shoulders and forced her, through the sheer command of his body language, to meet his eyes. Merry had the fleeting thought that she'd never had

an argument with a naked man and that it really wasn't
a fair way to fight.

The only sound in the room was the uneven pattern
of their breathing. She could feel her heartbeat quick-
ening as she waited for him to speak. He didn't. He just
looked into her eyes for a long while, his expression un-
readable, his hands firm on her upper arms. When he
lowered his mouth to hers, she wasn't surprised and yet
she didn't know what to think. Was he angry? Had she
hurt him? Was that what she'd meant to do?

But his lips were gently demanding and perhaps, a little rough in their pressure. She didn't even consider resisting, wasn't ready to let go when he ended the kiss, and
felt an aching loneliness when he drew away from her.
"There's nothing I can say that will make you believe me,
Merry. Arguing about emotion is pointless and unprod-
uctive. And after I leave, you'll probably be able to ra-
tionalize the attraction between us as a passing physical
need." His gaze never wavered from hers. She'd never
seen him so deadly serious. "I meant it last night when I
told you I was falling in love with you. I meant it then and
I mean it now. Fight it all you want, but last night
wouldn't have happened if you didn't feel the same way."

He took a deep breath. "Yes, I do want something from
you. A lot of somethings, in fact. I'm staying in Austin
to be near you and for no other reason. I've rented an
apartment and a car on a month-to-month lease. I've arranged to have some of my personal things sent from
California. I'm staying here, Merry. I'm going to write
my dissertation and spend as much time with you as
you'll allow."

"Write your dissertation and spend time with me?" She
repeated. "That appears to be a conflict of interest . . . or
are you simply killing two birds with one stone?"

"Appearances can be deceiving, Merry." He stepped past her and walked toward the bedroom.

She didn't know what else to do except follow. Lee had said he loved her. His lovemaking was convincing evidence. But was he staying in Austin to be near her or to be near Emerry? The possibilities wavered in her mind, nagged at her emotions. She watched as he dressed and experienced a painful longing to stop him. "Did Emee suggest you come to Austin?" The question came from nowhere, but Merry knew it had only been waiting for an opportunity to be voiced. "Have you talked to her about publishing your dissertation?"

Lee didn't pause. "I spoke with your mother once...no, twice. The first time, it was by telephone, the second time, I went to her home in Denver. That was two, maybe three, months ago. She told me both times that you absolutely refused to talk to anyone about your modeling career and that, for private reasons, she couldn't talk about it either. She gave me a glass of tea and offered to offer me the benefit of her experience and expertise in 'show business', as she called it. She asked a lot of questions about my research and seemed to know many of the people I've talked with in doing my research." He zipped up his jeans with one quick upward pull and buckled his belt. "All in all, I thought she was a charming and interesting woman. But I haven't communicated with her in any way since." He tossed Merry a perfunctory glance. "Believe it or not."

"Are you telling me she didn't call to let you know the number and time of my flight from Denver?"

His lips tightened for an instant. "It was an anonymous phone call, Merry. As far as I'm concerned, it still is."

Should she believe him? Was Emee capable of not in-terfering in the situation she'd created? Was Lee capable of looking her, Merry, straight in the eye and patently lying? "You have to admit it does look suspicious, Lee. You don't tell me who you are or what you're after until it's—" she swallowed, but couldn't catch the next words "—too late. You arrive in Austin on the same day I re-ceive this legal demand from my mother. She can be de-vious. I know her."

"Maybe you do. Or maybe you're too sensitive. What if she really wants to spend time with Molly and with you? You seem determined that *isn't* what she wants. Therefore you deny the possibility." He came to stand before her. "But I don't want to talk about your mother. I want to know if you're afraid of me."

How could she answer that? Merry stared up at him, searching her heart for a truthful reply. "No. I'm not afraid. Just cautious."

"Will you spend the day with me?"

It was a trap. She knew it, even as she nodded her consent.

He smiled then. A touching, tender smile. "Good. I'm hungry. How long will it take you to get ready? Or should I make another stab at cooking breakfast?"

"Don't do that. It'll only take me ten or fifteen min-utes. I'll call and ask Janie to have Molly ready when we get there."

"Good. Now that the smoke's cleared, I'll put the bat-tery back in the alarm."

With that, he left her alone in the bedroom. Left her to wonder if the smoke had really cleared or if she was walking straight into a blazing fire.

". . . OR I'LL HUFF AND I'LL PUFF and I'll blo-o-o-w your house down. . . ." Merry's voice dwindled to a somnolent whisper as Molly's head drooped against her mother's shoulder. Black curls framed an angelic face. Tiny lips, pursed in sleep, blew out little sighs. Merry gently eased the bedtime storybook from Molly's chubby grasp and then stroked her daughter's china doll cheeks with loving fingers.

Lee sat, mesmerized, by the picture of mother and daughter performing the bedtime ritual. He's listened to the expression in Merry's voice as she read. He'd watched Molly wage a futile battle with the sandman. And he knew he wanted to be a part of it every night for the rest of his life.

The strength of his desire surprised him, but he didn't doubt its staying power. An anonymous phone call might have put him beside Merry on that plane, but some guiding force had dialed his number. The emotions she evoked in him were like none he'd experienced before. He could neither explain them nor deny their existence. If this wasn't love, it was a damn fine imitation.

The only problem was whether or not Merry would come to care for him in the same way. Molly, he thought, wouldn't be a problem. After the day they'd spent together, he knew he could win her heart with a little time and effort. It was Merry who had him worried. Oh, she'd been happy enough to be with him. And at times, he'd been surprised by an odd wistfulness in her expression. But her veil of composure had been firmly in place. Lover or not, she would let him get only so close to her heart.

But he would remedy that, he thought. With a little time, a lot of patience, she would learn she could trust him. Even with her deepest secrets, her darkest fears.

When she stood, cradling Molly in her arms, he stood, too, and held out his arms. "Do you want me to carry her to bed?" he asked quietly.

"No, thanks." She started for the door. "I'll be back in a minute."

Lee nodded and waited for her to leave the room before he walked to the window. The sun had been gone for perhaps thirty minutes and twilight was beginning to give way to the night. It had been a hot, gorgeous day and Lee had enjoyed every moment of it. Merry had been uncomfortable some of the time. He'd noticed her nervous movements, knew she was looking at him, weighing his actions, measuring his words. It was time they talked, he decided.

Merry entered the room and a warm spiral of welcome wandered through him. He offered a slight smile. Her lips curved to match his in response. His heart jumped with the desire to hold her in his arms. His body tightened with an all too familiar longing. He calmed both and made his way to the sofa. When she joined him, he began to relax. Be careful, he warned himself. He had to know about her past, because not to know would rob him of a vital part of the woman he loved. Merry needed him, he knew that. But she also needed to talk.

"I'd like to tell you about my research." He dropped the statement like a bomb and waited to see whether or not it would explode in his face. "I think you should know why I came looking for you in the first place."

"Emerry," she said coolly. "You were looking for Emerry."

"Yes. You're right. Do you mind if we talk about it?"

She shifted a small, but significant distance away from him. "I'd prefer not to, but I suppose I'm not going to get a choice."

"You can ask me to leave."

"And if I did ask, would you go?"

"Yes."

The unequivocal word hung heavily in the silence. Lee knew her next request would either deny her feelings or admit them. He hoped for one, dreaded the other, but was ready to accept either. He could only do so much and if she wouldn't listen . . .

"What is it you want me to know?" she said an eternity later.

His relief came straight from the heart. "I want you to know about me. About my history, my background, and the reasons I chose child stars as the subject of my dissertation. I want you to understand why it was important that I find Emerry and why I didn't launch into an explanation the moment I boarded the plane. I had no intention of sitting beside you, but there you were and the next seat was empty and it seemed silly to pass up the opportunity."

"Were you so sure I was Emerry?"

"You haven't changed that much, Merry. Besides, I'd studied your photographs until there wasn't a detail of your face I didn't know by heart. From the beginning, you were the one who fascinated me. The others, well, they interested me, a couple of them truly held my attention. But you . . . I don't know how to explain it except that something in those photographs spoke to me. Or maybe it was the idea that while you seemed to have it all, you walked away from it."

"Walked away." Merry repeated the words softly, as if they surprised her. She tucked a slender foot under her and pulled one of the sofa pillows into her arms. "I'm not the first person to have left a successful career."

"No, but you're the only child celebrity I've found who left by choice. And it was your choice, wasn't it, Merry? You could have continued modeling if that's what you'd wanted."

She nodded. "It was my choice not to accept another contract."

"You won't tell me why, I suppose?"

A shadow darkened the blue of her eyes. "This is *your* confession, Lee. I never said I would participate in an exchange of information."

"No." He wished he hadn't asked the question, simply because it had brought the coolness back to her voice. But he couldn't monitor every word that came out of his mouth. He wouldn't do that, not even for her. "When I started college, a number of years ago, I roomed with a boy whose sister had committed suicide. Her name was Julie. She was fifteen and wanted to be a 'star'. She'd done a few commercials as a child, but adolescence had stripped her of camera appeal. So at fifteen, she ended her life because she thought her 'career' had peaked early and was over forever."

Lee clasped his hands between his knees and stared at the floor for a moment. "Julie's story has haunted me ever since I first heard it. I don't know why, but over the years, I've had a fascination for fame, however transient it might be, and its effects on the lives of the people it touches. I never really considered exploring any other topic for my dissertation."

"Why did you restrict it to just child celebrities?"

"For one thing, celebrity in and of itself is too broad a topic. And it seems obvious that a child of three or four or even older is not old enough to choose an acting or modeling career by himself. There has to be a catalyst. Either parents or an authority figure of some kind. How old were you when you did that first ad for Hamil and Harrison?"

"Six months."

"And who signed the contract on your behalf?"

The corners of her lips tightened with a frown. "Emee. But she's hardly the first 'stage mother' to push a child into show business. And I knew kids who loved it. You can't base your thesis on the idea that every child star was manipulated by someone else's ambition."

"No, that isn't my point at all. I'm interested in how fame affects the development of a child. If a six-month-old baby grows up in front of a camera, with the lavish attention of an adoring public, if she has money and travels and smiles on cue as a way of life, how does that affect the adult she becomes? And what if, as so often occurs, the fame isn't sustained into adult life? Is there a feeling of failure? Is it emotionally crippling?"

He leaned forward, eager for her to understand. And as he did, Merry found herself withdrawing. He was coming too close with his words, presenting ideas she understood all too well. After a minute, he continued with slightly less intensity.

"In this day and age, when so many parents are ambitious for themselves and their children, there seems to be a new influx of the 'stage mother' or 'stage father'. More parents are competing for the opportunity to put their little darling into the spotlight. I think it's a phenomenon that deserves study and attention."

"You could be on the talk-show circuit, Lee." Merry plucked at the rolled binding of the pillow she held. "I can see it all now. You and Emee on the Donahue show. That would be something to see."

He said nothing for a while and when he raised his gaze to hers, she knew he was disappointed by her cynicism.

"All right, Merry. You see my dissertation as an attempt to exploit children and to profit from society's appetite for glamour. I see it as a professional way of exploring one area in which we're pushing children to become adults earlier and faster than ever before. Child celebrities are only one extreme of an overall problem. I don't want to pick up the paper tomorrow morning and read about another Julie who thought she was a failure at fifteen."

"Neither do I, Lee." Merry turned slightly toward him, as she tucked several strands of dark hair behind her ear. "But I don't fit the profile. I've never considered myself a failure. Not at fifteen or twenty-five."

"It would be simplistic and wrong to say failure is the only consequence, Merry. You bear scars from your celebrity experience. You're still paying a price for the fame you knew as a child."

She couldn't argue with that. But she couldn't admit to it, either. One of her scars was disillusionment, and the price she continued to pay for it was the inability to easily trust other people. "Maybe so," she said quietly and firmly. "But I'm not going to open up my past for analysis and I don't want you to pressure me about doing so."

"I wasn't aware I was pressuring you."

"It's your profession, Lee. You might as well wear a neon sign around your neck proclaiming that you're a psychologist. You're always asking questions and putting me in a position where I say more than I intend to say. If this is going to work . . . if you're going to be hanging around here…" She paused to consider what she was saying and how far she was committing herself to him. Her heart tightened. The look in his eyes squeezed her like a sponge and a resigned and hopeful sigh slipped past her lips. "And I guess I am going to allow you to hang around, after all. But please don't ask me questions about my childhood. Not even indirect ones."

"Can I express any interest at all in who you were before you became Merry McLennan?"

"You already know about Emerry, Lee. I see no point in discussing her."

He pursed his lips in a disappointment Merry did not want to acknowledge. What on earth did he want from her? She'd agreed to see him, to spend time with him, to explore the attraction growing between them. Did he have to have information, too? Couldn't he just settle for what she was prepared to offer?

"All right, Merry. I'll do my best."

"One more thing."

His eyes lifted to hers and he waited for her to explain.

"I want . . . I'd like you to promise that you won't mention me in your dissertation. I really don't want to be included in any study."

The silence that followed seemed endless, but Merry didn't let her gaze waver from his. "I can't do that." He settled back against the sofa cushion, relaxed and determined. So determined. "I have to include Emerry Edwards in my paper. I have no more choice in the matter than you do. You were famous, Merry. And you disappeared. I can't *not* mention that. So with or without your approval, with or without your cooperation, Emerry will be included in this dissertation. I learned a great deal about you before we met and I won't ignore my own observations. I can promise you that nothing you've said to me will appear in the paper and nothing in it will intrude upon your privacy. Trust me, Merry. I won't disappoint you."

Every instinct told her he was sincere. A chorus of emotions rose up, urging her to trust him and to stop worrying. "Who will read this infamous dissertation?" she asked cautiously. "How can I be sure it won't wind up on some publisher's desk?"

"You can't be sure, Merry. All I can tell you is that I'm writing the paper to earn my degree. Period. A panel of professors will read it, evaluate it, and pass judgment on it . . . and me. After that . . . well, it'll probably go in my desk drawer or maybe on the bookshelf. I have no plans to submit it to any publisher, but you're just going to have to take my word for that."

She knew it would be futile to protest further. It all boiled down to trust and although a part of her longed to cast caution aside, another part warned her to proceed slowly. "Is your word good, Lee?"

A sensual smile took his mouth by degrees. "Every bit as good as the rest of me. Maybe better."

She smiled, too, and somehow, miraculously she felt at ease. When he scooted forward, she scooted to meet him halfway and they tumbled back onto the sofa in a carefree manner she couldn't have imagined only five minutes before. His lips nestled into the hollow below her ear and feathery sensations burst with splendor beneath her skin. She was a lunatic, she thought. She must be. How else could she be taking such a chance with him?

But when his kiss grazed her throat and moved up to seal her lips and her fate, she didn't feel as if she were taking any chance at all. He felt very certain, very real in her arms, and any question of risk seemed petty and intrusive, unworthy of consideration. Sweet whispers of passion whisked away rational thought and Merry let herself drift into the warm haven of Lee's caress.

When his hands slipped beneath the hem of her blouse, she sighed, knowing she would have to stop him. Soon. There was little chance that Molly would awaken, but it was possible. And Merry was always conscious of her daughter's welfare. Much as she wanted Lee with her, in her bed . . . and inside her, she couldn't let him stay. Not tonight. Not with Molly in the house. But, oh, his touch felt so good. So warm. So loving. She wondered if it were possible to drown in pleasure. It must be. How else could she be suffocating with just the gentle stroke of his thumb on her breast and the teasing play of his tongue against hers?

Moment slipped into pleasurable moment and when she realized Lee was pulling away from her, she clung to him. He didn't need to change position, she thought. He felt perfect lying next to her. "Where are you going?" she asked as she pressed an inviting kiss to the underside of his chin.

He propped himself on one elbow and gazed into her hungry eyes. "I'm going to my apartment. I think it's now or never. Otherwise, tomorrow morning, you may have a hard time explaining to Molly what I'm doing in your bed."

"I could tell her you came over to burn her breakfast."

His smile was gentle. His thoughtfulness of Molly and of her impressionable age touched Merry more than she could say. She raised her fingertip to trace the line of his face from temple to chin.

He caught her hand and kissed the fingertip . . . then all the others. "As I said, it's now or never. May I see you tomorrow?"

She nodded and felt another sigh push at her throat when he stood up and pulled her into a sitting position.

"Call me," she said and realized how vulnerable she sounded.

"Yes." He took her hand and led her to the front door. Gathering her into his arms, he held her close, then released her with only the promise of a kiss. "Good night, Merry. Don't let the big bad wolf worry you. There's nothing to be afraid of. Remember, the three little pigs lived happily ever after."

"It's Molly's favorite story."

"And Willie's, too." He hesitated, gave her lips one more wistful kiss, then left.

She closed the door and leaned against it. All right, she thought, so she hadn't exercised much control during the past twenty-four hours. That only proved she was human. Still, it would take more than a few blissful moments of physical gratification to convince her she had nothing to worry about and no reason to be afraid.

Her lips felt warm with recollection. It had been a pleasant day. For herself. For Molly. Lee seemed to complete some missing link in their lives. He had just walked in and *fit*, somehow. But that didn't mean anything. It was no reason to forget the lessons she'd learned early and painfully. People weren't always what they appeared to be. If Lee wanted to stick around and prove himself, then she could accept that. Time would tell if there really was such a thing as "happily ever after."

12

SUMMER WEATHER lingered through September and into October. So did Lee. Page by page, his dissertation grew. Hour by hour, he fell more in love with Merry. He sometimes daydreamed about the three of them, he, Merry and Molly, as a family. But he didn't mention those thoughts to Merry and he didn't press her for a commitment, although as he got closer to completion of his research paper, he wondered how he could return to California without her.

As a counselor, he'd been trained to see both sides of a problem. But with Merry, he didn't, couldn't understand why she kept him at a distance. As a lover, she was everything and more than he could have asked for. It was as if, when they were alone in the dark, she relinquished her doubts and came to him without reservation. But the rest of the time, she maintained a barrier that kept him from asking the wrong questions and kept her from revealing things she'd decided he had no right to know.

It was even more frustrating to realize that he had enough material about Emerry in his dissertation, but didn't know nearly enough about her for his own personal satisfaction. Emerry stood in the middle of his relationship with Merry and he couldn't get her to budge. That Merry kept her alter ego there for a reason, Lee didn't doubt. She was afraid to trust him and his research provided a buffer. He knew that, but didn't know how to get around it.

Merry seldom mentioned her mother and so Lee didn't, either. The one time he had asked about Emee and her request to visit her granddaughter, Merry had said she'd seen an attorney and wasn't overly concerned about the threat of any legal action. The lawyer, she'd said, had taken care of writing a reply. Lee was pretty certain, though, that there had been no contact between mother and daughter since the letter incident and he felt sure the cold war continued.

Even so, it was Emee who precipitated the showdown with Merry. Although Lee knew that sooner or later he and Merry would have to discuss their relationship and the future, he hadn't planned on having the discussion until he'd completed the dissertation. But one afternoon, on her way to pick up Molly at the sitter's, Merry stopped by to see Lee. She'd finished at the clinic a little earlier than usual and thought he might like to go with her to get Molly and then, perhaps, the three of them could catch an early movie.

Lee liked the idea and asked her to wait while he changed clothes. And then, with eerie timing, the phone rang. Lee picked it up in the living room, but it wouldn't have mattered. Merry could have heard his half of the conversation wherever he'd been in the small apartment. He toyed with the idea of not telling her that Emee had been the caller. But he didn't want to be accused later of concealing information, so after he'd concluded the call by jotting down a phone number and promising to return it at a later time, he turned to Merry with a resigned look on his face.

"That was your mother."

She looked surprised. "Why was she calling *you*?"

"She asked me to meet her tomorrow." He glanced at the scratch pad. "Did you know she was in Austin?"

"Yes. She called me this afternoon, too. We talked briefly. I was very busy." Merry frowned. "But you didn't answer my question. Why was she calling you?"

He didn't like the tone of her voice, but decided to answer anyway. "I told you. She asked me to meet her at the Four Seasons Hotel tomorrow. Apparently, she's staying there."

"Yes." Merry let the quiet stretch for a moment. "Why does she want to meet with you? How did she even know how to reach you, Lee?"

"I don't know. Maybe she called the information operator. Maybe she called my California number and got this number from the recording. Does it matter?"

"That probably depends on *why* she called."

"She said she had an idea she thought would interest me and she wants to discuss it."

"What kind of idea?" The suspicion was there, now. In her words. In her eyes.

"It wasn't about you."

"I find that hard to believe." Merry crossed her arms beneath her breasts. "You may as well tell me, Lee. Whatever scheme the two of you have cooked up, Emee won't be able to keep quiet about it. She'll tell me. Sooner or later."

Anger sluiced through him in ice-cold waves. Dammit, he hadn't done anything wrong. He didn't deserve this. He flung his hand out toward the phone. "Be my guest, Merry. Call your mother. The phone number's right there. Call her and find out just what the *two of us have cooked up!*"

"You can hardly blame me, Lee, for being angry. You knew how I felt about the two of you collaborating."

"*Collaborating*? *I* answered my phone, Merry. I listened until I had the opportunity to ask if I could return the call at a more convenient time. Why in hell would you assume I'm collaborating with Emee?"

Her lips tightened, but she didn't answer his question. "You're going to meet her tomorrow, aren't you?"

"Yes, I probably am."

Silence reigned for one accusing moment. "What if I ask you not to?"

"Don't ask." He said the words with deadly calm. "I won't buckle to your insecurities, Merry. No matter how much I care about you."

"Care about exploiting me, you mean."

His face froze with renewed anger. "Do you want to explain that remark?"

She looked at him then, squarely, and her heart pounded fast and hard as she realized how carelessly, thoughtlessly, she had accused him. "You're writing about me. Emee wants you to publish what you write. What else could she want to discuss with you?"

"Yes. What else?" He raked a hand through his hair. "It all boils down to one thing for you, doesn't it? Everyone who professes to love you must want something other than your love in return. Because your mother contacts me, you immediately assume I've been conspiring with her. Why would you jump to that conclusion, Merry? I've given you every reason to trust me. Every reason in the world."

"You deceived me from the beginning, Lee. From the moment we met. You should have told me then who you were and what you wanted."

"Maybe I should have. Maybe I shouldn't. But I do know I've been paying for that omission ever since. The blame isn't all mine, though, Merry. If you hadn't been so afraid of your own feelings, you'd have asked questions about me, my background, my history. You didn't do that. You even tried very hard to forget my name."

"Oh, so it's my fault you didn't tell the truth?"

"No, Merry. I think it has to do with Emerry, the person you left behind. You're afraid to trust me. Not because of anything I've done, but because somewhere in your past something painful made you decide never to trust anyone, never to allow anyone the power to hurt you again. Maybe it was your mother who hurt you. I don't know. As a psychologist, I do know you're going to have to face that past at some time in your life, whether it's now or later."

Her breath hung in her throat. Anger...or maybe recollected pain pressed tightly at her chest. "It would be better for you if that time were now, wouldn't it, Lee? I could just sit down here, open a vein, and bleed out my history for your precious book. You'd like that, wouldn't you? You and Emee, both."

He stepped toward her and stopped. His eyes reflected a mixture of frustration and pain. She saw it and didn't know how to overcome her own emotions to salvage his. She'd accused him falsely. Somehow, she knew that, but some deeply ingrained fear forced her to attack him, forced her to push him until he *proved* her accusation wasn't true. She trembled with the risk she was taking, but could not stop the doubts that bathed her logic in suspicion. When he spun on his heel and entered the bedroom, she was more afraid than she'd ever been. What 'if her mistrust was more than he could handle? What if he stopped loving her because of it?

He returned, a sheaf of paper in his hand. "Here, Merry. This is the dissertation. Read it. Then come back and tell me how I've exploited you. Tell me then how you can't trust me. If the past weeks haven't convinced you of my love, then maybe this will. And if it doesn't—" he lowered his voice to a quiet, weary baritone "—if it doesn't, you can sleep with your suspicions for the rest of your life. I can't do any more."

Her hand shook, trembling with the need to take the proof he offered, but she forced herself not to reach for it. To do so would kill some fundamental dignity inside him. He wouldn't feel quite the same toward her again. Not if she took the dissertation. Not if she accepted proof of his honesty.

No. She had to come to grips with her "insecurities," as Lee had called them. She had to decide to trust him despite her fear of betrayal. Not because Lee had proved himself worthy, but because she loved him enough to accept his words as truth. Simple. And yet, the very idea scared her to the core of her being. She had to get away, had to think. "I have to get Molly." She spun toward the door. "I . . . I'll—" The words wouldn't come. No explanation would suffice.

She opened the door and raced through it, slamming it behind her and running. Running down the steps. Running toward her car. Running as she'd been doing for the past eight years.

Suddenly, a flash of insight struck her with the force of a heavy fall. But she hadn't fallen. She stood beside her car . . . and realized she was still running. Running from the past. Running from a confrontation with Emee. Running from the man she loved. Running to nowhere.

It was a sobering thought.

LEE PACED THE LENGTH of the apartment twice, then changed direction and walked the width three times. He fought the impulse to follow Merry and, somehow, persuade her to reason. But he was too hurt, too angry, to make much sense now. Besides, he knew it was better for her to work this out on her own. He debated about phoning Emee, but couldn't believe that would accomplish anything other than satisfying his curiosity. What was going on between Emee and Merry, anyway? And how had he gotten in the middle of it?

He picked up the dissertation and leafed through the pages. Why hadn't she taken it, read it, and realized he was innocent of deception? It would have proven he hadn't exploited their relationship. Yet, in a way, he was glad she'd refused. It hurt not to be trusted, but to have to be exonerated from guilt . . . well, that bothered him some, too.

He flipped to the last few sheets, the ones he'd written that afternoon, and began to read. The work was good, the research thorough. He wished he could have included more about Merry, but he had kept his word and left her privacy intact. He didn't feel the paper suffered because of it, but God knew that *he* had. How could she have believed, even for an instant, that he would conspire against her? And with her mother.

Which brought him back to the beginning. What had Emee done to inspire such distrust in her own daughter? As far as he had been able to tell, from the one face-to-face encounter he'd had with Emee, she was ambitious and an attention seeker. But she also had charm and a certain finesse that kept her from seeming too abrasive. And it had been obvious to him within five minutes of meeting her that she sincerely loved her daughter and wanted the best for her. Even if she didn't understand what really was best.

He put down the dissertation and paced the room again. What good did it do to study human behavior, if he couldn't understand the behavior of the one person he loved? And what did any of it matter if Merry didn't come back?

Reluctantly, he went back to the research paper and carried it into the bedroom. He'd work while he waited to hear from Merry. If she didn't call by nine o'clock, he'd call her. If she wouldn't talk to him by phone, he'd go in person. Tonight, he decided, they would settle this. Settle the issue of trust. Settle the future of their relationship.

He turned on the computer and hoped he wouldn't have to settle for a finished dissertation and a string of empty tomorrows.

MERRY SPENT THE BETTER PART of two hours sitting in her parked car outside Lee's apartment. She stared at the large entrance sign which advertised apartments for rent by the day, the week, or the month, but she was oblivious to her surroundings, unaware of the passage of time. The past she'd tried so hard to escape had caught her. All the running had led her back to the beginning.

She'd thought about it, made herself take a good, long look at what she'd left behind and where she was today. She tried to be objective, tried to assess when caution had become a barrier against the world. When had she started to see all but a handful of relationships as threatening? She knew she hadn't started that way. So how had she come to accuse Lee of exploiting her?

She was in love with him. Hopelessly, completely. She'd known it for weeks, now. If she were honest, she'd have to admit her heart belonged to him long before she'd left Galveston Island. So how could she have attacked him as she'd done only a little while ago? Was it Emee's presence in Austin that brought back the insecurities? Or was it something more?

There were dozens of questions, but no answers. Only a sense of discovery, of new perspective and fresh insights. She had a long way to go, Merry realized. But at last, she had faced her fear and knew that she could overcome it.

She reached for the door handle, intending to carry an apology and her new insight upstairs to Lee. But a glance at her watch changed her mind. She had to pick up Molly. It was past five already and she'd planned on getting her early, today. How could she have been so lost in thought that she'd failed to think of her daughter? Just another indication of her state of mind and her need to deal with the emotions she'd buried so many years before.

She started the car, sent Lee a silent promise of her imminent return, and drove straight to the sitter's house. Surprise registered on the sitter's face when she opened the door to Merry's knock. She explained that Molly had left more than an hour before with her grandmother. The sitter was sure Merry knew about it. Emee had said she'd left word at the clinic and Molly was so happy to see her "Nina." It was all right, wasn't it?

Merry reassured the woman as best she could over the tension in her own throat. It wasn't the sitter's fault. Not really. Emee had picked up Molly one other time, months and months ago, but the sitter, obviously, had remembered. In any case, Emee could be most convincing.

Merry left, after further assurances to the sitter, and sat in her car, trying to figure out where to begin looking for her mother and her daughter. What was Emee up to? Had she mentioned picking up Molly when she and Merry had spoken earlier? Try as she might, Merry couldn't recall. She'd been annoyed that Emee was in town, annoyed that she'd interrupted her lunch, annoyed because the two of them couldn't have a simple conversation without Emee bringing in a bunch of why-don't-yous and if-only-you'd-let-mes.

But what had she said about Molly? Think.

Merry couldn't think. A slow panic was roiling inside her. She knew Molly was safe. Emee would never hurt her. Not physically anyway. What if she was filling Molly's head with stories of glamour and glitz? Telling her how she could be the envy of every little girl in America?

Merry jerked the car into gear. She would go to Lee. The situation needed a hero. And he was the only candidate she knew.

"CALM DOWN." he told her for the fiftieth time. "You're overreacting. This is your mother, Merry. Molly's grandmother. Why are you so panic-stricken?"

She wondered that, herself, but the feeling wouldn't subside. She had always known exactly where Molly was, exactly what she was doing at any given moment. Whenever Emee had been with Molly, Merry had been right there to supervise and, if necessary, to intervene. She was used to being in control and now that Emee had usurped that control, however innocently, Merry was shaken. She didn't know what to do.

Luckily, Lee had more perspective. "I called the hotel and there's no answer in Emee's room. Do you think she might have picked up Molly and taken her home? Is it possible she left a message for you at the clinic?"

"I don't know. Maybe. I did leave early."

"Let's go to your house, Merry. If they're not there already, they're bound to show up eventually."

Merry hoped he was right, but fought another round of panic when she walked into her empty house. Lee said nothing, but opened his arms and Merry walked straight into them, feeling comforted and reassured just in having him with her. As always when he touched her, desire spiraled through her veins in warm, honeyed waves. Even now, even with the worry, she experienced it and marveled at the response Lee evoked in her.

She had loved Ian for his kindness, his love of life, but she realized now that she had not given herself to him completely. He'd been a friend, a refuge, but not her lover... not in the sense that Lee was her lover. She belonged with Lee in a way she'd never known before and would never know again. She accepted that as he held her tight against his chest, and as his heart beat with the rhythm of her own.

"I love you, Lee." Her whispered confession came unannounced, but long overdue. His arms tightened around her and she felt his sigh slip past her cheek with warm pleasure. But there was more to tell, and he deserved to know everything. "This afternoon after I left you, I had a moment of revelation. As I ran down the steps, I realized I was running away. From you. From the past. From Emee. From everything. Even when I married Ian, I think I was just trying to run from one identity to another. I never fully understood that Emerry *is* a part of me. I can't escape that. I should never have tried."

Lee drew back to look at her. "Does this mean I'm no longer under suspicion of conspiracy?" A somber smile crinkled the corners of his eyes. "Don't answer that, yet. Tell me instead why you were running away."

"You can probably explain it better than I can."

"It's important that you put it into your own words."

She frowned. "You sound like a psychologist, Lee. Besides, how can I talk about this when I don't know where my mother has taken my daughter or what the two of them are doing?"

"That's precisely why it's on your mind, Merry. Molly is safe. She'll be returned to you soon. Logically, you know that. But you're not in control at the moment. Your mother is. And something in you ... a memory perhaps ... can't handle that. It makes you fearful and angry."

He was right. Those emotions stirred inside her even as he named them. And her memory began to toss out bits and pieces of old resentments. "She always loved being in control," Merry said slowly, remembering and trying to sort out the truth. "Emee *loved* the contract meetings. She'd talk for weeks about what the company executives would offer, and how she'd haggle over the amount of money, only to win some other contract point. Perks, she called them. Extras. She never asked me what *I* wanted. I was never included in any of the meetings, not even when I was old enough to understand. She managed to convince everyone she spoke for me." Merry jammed her hands into her sweater pockets and moved away from Lee. He was her center, though, and she didn't go too far away.

"Did you tell anyone you wanted a say in your future?"

"No." Merry scoffed at her own omission. "I was in awe of Emee and a little frightened by her ambition. How do you tell your own mother that you don't want the life she's *sacrificed* to give you? And that's the way Emee saw it ... still sees it. She did everything for me. Even when I had to buy my way out of the career, she said she was taking the money to help me. I'd need it later, she told me."

Merry glanced at Lee. "I guess I should explain that. On my eighteenth birthday, I signed over all the assets I'd accrued during my career. All of them except the money I needed to attend college. Emee took it without blinking an eye, telling me it was mine for the asking, later, after I'd come to my senses and realized what I'd thrown away. She signed an agreement that she'd never reveal where I was or anything about Emerry Edwards other than what was public knowledge at the time. As far as I know, she kept the agreement, until she contacted you. Of course, since she made the call anonymously, she feels she did nothing wrong." Merry grimaced and rubbed the frown that wrinkled her forehead. "Emee can always shift the blame, too. She's very good at that."

"I'm sure it was hard to deal with the idea that your mother would take all the money you'd earned over the years." Lee's comment was nonjudgmental and Merry loved him for trying to put her at ease.

"By that time, I was pretty inured to Emee's unmotherly traits. Or maybe I was simply tired of trying to be who she wanted me to be and not who I really was." Merry knew she had to say more, dig out the dirt, but, oh, she hated to do so. "It wasn't easy growing up in the limelight. I never liked it. There was so much pressure to perform, to be on stage. And the only time I felt important was when I was in front of the camera.

"For my eleventh birthday, Emee arranged a big party at the company's offices. Some really famous people came and the news media covered it. Emee said it was wonderful publicity. But she hadn't had time to get a present for me. One of the PR men told me it was lucky my birthday happened to be on the same day that a highly-publicized movie was opening in town. You can imagine how special I felt.

"But the more times things like that happened, the more reserved I became. And everyone liked it. They told me how mature I was, that I was so 'in control'. So I learned how to wear a mask, to keep my feelings locked away and bring them out only for the camera. Not much risk of getting hurt that way." Merry sighed. "I still might have been all right, if it hadn't been for Emee's determination to keep me in the public eye as a celebrity, over and above the ads I did for the company."

Merry lifted a trembling hand to her temple. She was uncomfortable telling Lee all this. She was uncomfortable remembering it at all. "At thirteen, I looked older than my age and she decided it would be good for me to date some of the attractive young men who were destined to be tomorrow's stars of stage and screen. I don't know how, but Emee knew who they were and she knew how to persuade them that being seen with me would be great publicity. Of course, I quickly learned that the young men weren't only interested in getting their pictures in a tabloid and I ended up fighting off their advances. Emee could never understand why I resisted going out on these 'dates'. She told me not to be so fussy. He—whoever it happened to be at the time—could do me a lot of good, she'd say. Then she'd ask me if I realized how lucky I was to have the opportunities to go out with real stars. Did I know how many girls would die for the chances I so callously rejected?

"So I learned how to control the situations Emee forced me into. I dated, but I mastered the art of the cold shoulder and, surprisingly, I received more vows of undying devotion than ever before." She met Lee's gaze directly. "A lot of men have said they loved me, but I knew they loved the image of Emerry, the Sunshine Girl, America's sweetheart. Even Ian, I think, felt a little that way." She hesitated. "You're the only one I've actually ever considered believing."

Lee swallowed his emotion and smiled encouragement. "Keep on believing, Merry. I intend to stick around for a very long time, always declaring *my* undying devotion."

She walked to the window and pulled aside the curtain. "Why aren't they here yet? It's almost six-thirty."

"They'll be here. Tell me the rest, Merry. Finish it."

With a sigh, she let the curtain fall into place, but kept her back to him. "When I was sixteen, Emee decided it was time to break with the Sunshine contracts and try for a movie role. As always, she took my agreement for granted and she proceeded to court a Hollywood producer. At the same time, she buddied up to the senior vice president of Hamil and Harrison, so he would release me from the contract when the movie offer came through. He'd been around since my first contract with the company and he'd been so nice to me. I had a lot of respect for him and thought he was great. I never suspected he . . ."

The words faded, the hurt she'd felt all those years ago returned. "When Emee approached him about the new contract he was eager to help . . . for a price. I was young, pretty, and finally—he thought—mature enough for a sophisticated relationship. He and Emee worked out a trade. Release from the contract for my . . . attention."

Her voice faltered there and Lee came up to stand behind her, his hands strong and caring on her shoulders. "Oh, Merry," he said, lending the words a measure of his sympathy and concern. For a moment or two, neither of them said anything, then Lee's grip on her tightened. "Are you sure Emee understood the nature of the . . . trade?"

"I'm sure. We never spoke about it, but she set up a contract negotiation meeting—the first, by the way, to which I was invited—and then, at the last minute, she couldn't make it. She called and told me it was important that I go and that I do whatever was necessary to please Marc—his name doesn't matter. He died a couple of years ago." A cynical laugh irritated her throat. "Emee sent flowers."

Lee didn't want to push, but he knew Merry had to take the final step, voice the pain and then, then she could begin to put it behind her. "What happened at the meeting?"

She shook her head, sending the raven-wing hair cascading forward to hide her face. "He all but raped me. He was alone in the office and I knew at once that something was wrong. But I'd known him so long and never thought . . . anyway, he was quick to tell me my mother approved and he was willing to help me get the movie role I wanted, if I was *nice* to him. It was like a scene from a B-movie. I laughed at him and . . . he slapped me. Then he started kissing me and touching . . ." She rubbed a finger across her lips, trying to wipe away the memory. "You get the picture, I'm sure. He probably would have succeeded with the rape if I hadn't pretended to see the error of my ways and agreed to cooperate. Then, at the last minute, I ran. And ran. And ran."

Anger flooded Lee with such intensity he had to clutch one hand with the other to keep from putting it through the wall. He'd expected something like this, and yet he was unprepared for his own emotional response. "I'm sorry, Merry. That must have been a terrible disillusionment." He pulled her back against him, and cradled her trembling body in the shelter of his embrace. He didn't know what else to do.

"You know—" her voice was husky and raw "—I thought I'd dealt with it. I really thought I had it under control. I never told anyone. Not even Ian. It took a long time to bring myself to trust him and even then, I couldn't find the words to tell him why it did take so long. He was always kind, very much a father figure for me. But I didn't tell him. I've never told anyone . . . before."

"What about your mother?"

Merry shrugged. "Oh, after Emee finally arrived home that night and gave me a ridiculous excuse for missing the meeting, she asked how it went. I told her I'd decided I didn't want to do a movie and I told her I didn't want to model anymore, either. That shook her up so badly, she forgot everything else. She got on the phone immediately and began rebuilding the bridges she thought I'd burned. The senior VP wasn't overly anxious to talk to her. I suppose he thought I'd told her what had happened and he might be facing a felony charge. Whether he was relieved to find she wanted to renew my contract or whether he was trying to buy my silence, he assured her I could work for Hamil and Harrison as long as I wanted. That was all she cared about. And she never said anything else to me about that night."

Merry shivered and Lee tightened his hold. "For my part, I tried to forget what had happened, how Emee must have set it up. I decided I could survive until I was eighteen and old enough to leave. The funny thing is she was totally shocked when I told her that I was leaving modeling. Not just the Sunshine contract, but all of it. She had no idea I was so unhappy."

Merry kept her head pressed against his shoulder and he simply held her until the emotion passed. When she pulled away, he steadied her. "You had a series of disillusionments, Merry. Especially at such a young age. It's no wonder you're so cautious about trusting other people."

"No, I suppose it isn't."

He studied her for a moment, assessing her ability to handle another question. "I think you should consider one thing, though. Is it possible that your mother doesn't know about the attempted-rape? Are you sure her excuse for not being at that meeting wasn't legitimate? Maybe the guy arranged for her to be somewhere else while he made his play for you." He held up a hand to quiet her protest. "It might be stretching your credibility, Merry, but it's a question that has to be asked. You know it does."

"She wouldn't answer truthfully, even if I did find the courage to ask her."

"Then you'll have to deal with that when it happens. But blaming her without proof is damaging to both of you. You need either to sever your relationship with her or forgive her and go on with your life."

"Easy for you to say."

"Yes, and difficult as hell to do. I know. I'll do all I can to help."

"Thank you. This has been quite an exper—" Outside a car door slammed and Merry ran to the front door. In a matter of minutes, Molly was in her arms, chattering like the happy, carefree child she was.

"Mommy, Mommy. Nina and me went to the park. I swinged and slided and—" her smile clouded with concern as she looked down "—and Willie pushed me and I fell in the dirt and tore my sock."

Merry offered appropriate assurances and Molly hugged her. "Willie was naughty and wouldn't let Nina take his picture."

"Did Nina take your picture?" Merry asked even as her gaze went to the doorway and Emee. "Hello, Mother. I've been worried."

"I left a message for you at that clinic. If you'd take a minute of your time to speak with me, Emerry, you wouldn't have to worry. All I wanted was to spend a little time with my grandchild." Emee breezed into the room like a strong wind, taking charge with the vitality of her presence. She set her purse on the table and looked around the room with interest. Her expression changed to curious pleasure when she saw Lee. "Hello, Mr. Zurbaron, isn't it? What a surprise to find you at my daughter's home. Are you going to be able to meet with me tomorrow?"

Lee's glance winged to Merry. "That depends, Mrs. Edwards, on what you want to discuss with me. I can tell you right now that I have no intention of offering my dissertation to your publisher friend. Merry wants to maintain her privacy and I respect her wish."

Emee frowned at her daughter. "I don't understand why privacy is so important to you, Merry. If you were a natural person, you'd want to—but that's neither here nor there. I also respect your wishes. Quite reluctantly, I might add." She turned again to Lee. "No, Mr. Zurbaron . . . may I call you Lee? . . . I have another project to offer you. My publisher friend has suggested that I might want to put together a book about modeling, based on my personal experience in managing Merry's career." She lifted her hand in a long-fingered dismissal of Merry's immediate protest. "Not to worry, dear, *you* will not be mentioned, except that I am your mother and

I did manage your career. That's only fair, I'd say. I don't know why I didn't think of the idea myself. It's perfect for me. But, unfortunately, I don't know any writers and I'm not sure how to begin a project of this magnitude. So I thought perhaps you, Lee, might be interested in helping me."

Lee was somewhat surprised by Emee's forceful presentation of the idea. No wonder Merry was always on her guard. "I don't think I'm the man for the job, since I'm a psychologist, not a writer. And I'm going to be very busy during the next few weeks, finishing my dissertation and then setting up a practice here in Austin. I'll have to make a couple of trips back and forth to the Coast. But perhaps I could put you in touch with someone who would be interested in ghostwriting for you."

"A ghostwriter?" Emee seemed uncertain if she needed that much help. Then she shrugged. "Oh, well, give me his name."

"Austin?" Merry said softly, tentatively. "You're going to stay in Austin?"

His lips curved in reply, his eyes promised Merry they would discuss it at length later. His reply was for Emee. "I'll have to check with *her* first, but I'll let you know. So, I guess there's really no need for us to meet tomorrow."

Emee seemed to consider that an unnecessary point as she walked to the sofa and elegantly took a seat. "Now, Merry, was there something you wanted to discuss with me?"

Merry lowered Molly to the floor. "As a matter of fact, Emee, you and I are going to discuss quite a number of things, beginning with your picking up Molly without my permission."

"I'm her grandmother and I did leave word. It isn't my fault you refuse to talk to me." For the first time, Emee looked uncomfortable. "That's why I hired that lawyer. If you'd answer my phone calls, I wouldn't have to resort to such tactics. Oh, and I know you're going to throw a fit about this, but I had a photographer take Molly's picture in the park today. And before you say anything, it's a picture for me, personally. I am her grandmother, you know, and I haven't a single professional shot to carry in my purse. I know you don't want her *exploited*, as you call it, although I don't know why you're so blind about this subject. Molly is a natural, every bit as good as you were, Merry, but—" again, the hand went into the air in a gesture of dramatic dismissal "—as I said, I respect your wishes on that. I don't understand them, but I've managed to keep my opinion to myself for eight years now. I guess I can manage to for a few more."

Merry sighed audibly and ignored Emee's explanations. "Lee? Would you take Molly out for a while? Maybe get her some dinner? I think it's time Emee and I had a serious conversation. You and Molly would only be bored, so would you—?"

"I'd be delighted." He turned to the child. "Molly, would you like to go out for pizza?"

Molly seconded the idea with enthusiasm. "Can Willie come? Pizza's his fav'rite."

"Mine, too." Lee reached for Molly's hand and offered all his support to Merry in a reassuring squeeze of her shoulder. "We'll be back in a couple of hours," he said. "Take care of yourself."

"I will." She drew a deep breath and thanked him with a look. "I'm in control now."

Lee left, reluctantly, hoping for her sake and his own, that she was right.

13

WHEN LEE RETURNED WITH MOLLY, Merry was alone. The house seemed dark, even though the kitchen and hallway were lit. Lee flicked on a lamp as Merry guided Molly toward a late bath and **bed.** He smiled to himself as he listened to Molly's endless string of questions and sleepy chatter. The smile faded a bit, though, when he heard her ask about her grandmother. Merry's answer was too soft to make out and he wondered if he should have left Merry and Emee alone as he had. Merry had relived a traumatic memory and then, to face her mother so soon. . . .

At least, she'd survived. And she loved him. She'd admitted it just a few hours ago. He only hoped she'd meant it. Restlessly, he made his way into the kitchen and sought out a bottle of wine and two glasses. He wasn't sure who needed it more . . . he or Merry. Merry, of course, he thought. His state of mind was uneven, nervous, but nothing compared to what hers must be. Making love was out of the question tonight but— damn—he ached to love away her pain and her past.

"You missed your favorite bedtime story, Willie," a soft voice said behind him.

A flickering heat began low in his groin and he tried to bank the fire before it got out of hand. Turning, he offered her a drink from his glass. "I'm sorry to hear that," he said. "Did I miss the 'huffing and puffing' part?"

Merry took a sip of the cool wine. "We didn't make it that far. Molly was asleep before the second little pig left home to seek his fortune."

"Oh." Lee drank in the sight of her. Merry had combed her black hair and tied it back at her nape. She wore no makeup and he thought he detected a trace of tears on the thickness of her eyelashes. He loved her so much he thought he would choke with the need to say the words. There was, he thought, little resemblance between the woman who stood before him now and the photographs he'd studied for so long. There was just as slight a resemblance between the dispassionate, objective researcher he had been and the passionate, committed lover he had become. Or maybe it was just that he'd learned to see with his heart. Either way, whether she called herself Emerry Edwards or Merry McLennan, he loved this woman deeply and forever. And he longed to tell her.

"Are you all right?" he asked instead.

"Yes. I had that talk with my mother." Merry cupped the goblet in the palm of her hand and twisted it so that the wine swirled to the rim. "She denied it, Lee. She said she'd gotten a message that night to meet with a movie producer and that she'd told Marcus—the senior vice president—to postpone our meeting, but he said he'd entertain me. Maybe take me out to dinner. She had no idea that wasn't what happened. And she couldn't imagine why I'd suddenly gone crazy and decided to throw away my career. She seemed genuinely shocked when I told her what really happened." The wine made another circle inside the glass. "I'm not sure if I can believe her."

Lee waited, guessing that Merry had already made the choice to forgive Emee for past mistakes, whether real or imagined. She just needed some time to heal her own wounds first. "She's a very forceful person," he said.

The corners of Merry's mouth tipped slightly. "That's one way of putting it, I suppose. She's been that way all my life and it's a sure bet she's not going to change, now."

"Maybe when she starts working on the 'how-to-be-a-model' book, she'll leave you alone."

"Oh, I'm sure she will for a while. Then she'll be back, stir up another tempest and move on to the next project. I'm just concerned about her influence on Molly."

"Molly will be fine," he stated simply and sincerely. "You're her anchor and regardless of what Emee does, Molly is going to grow up secure in her identity. She may want to model when she's older, but that will be her choice, Merry. Not anyone else's."

"Emee has set up a trust fund for Molly. She told me it was apparent I wasn't going to see the error of my ways and return to modeling and since I was really too old for it now anyway, she decided to put the money in Molly's name. She even offered to put my name on as trustee, in case I didn't trust her to manage the account for Molly." Merry stopped, shook her head wistfully, and raised puzzled eyes to meet Lee's. "I didn't have an answer for her. I've always thought of Emee as someone who would sell my soul for her own benefit, but now...well, I don't know. Maybe I did misjudge her."

"I expect it's going to take you a long time to decide the answer to that, Merry. I hope it won't take nearly as long to decide that you'll marry me."

"Marry you?" The shadows fled as happiness dawned in her eyes.

"Yes." He had to steady his voice before he continued. Had he ever been so uncertain before? Or so hopeful? "Merry-as-in-Christmas, will you marry, as-in-forever, me?"

She opened her mouth, closed it, again. "Are you sure, Lee? I mean, do you really want to move to Austin? I'd hate to leave the clinic, but I could find work in California, if you—"

"I like Austin. And just think . . . we'll be so close to Galveston and the Gulf."

She smiled at that. "You'll finish your degree first?"

"In as short a time as I can manage. The dissertation is all but finished now and I'll probably send it in for evaluation by the end of the month. I'll have to fly back to defend it and to pack my things, but you and Molly can go along, meet my family, 'see the sea'. We could get married there. My parents would love it and . . . you can invite Emee. Ken and Janie, too. In fact, invite anyone you want. Just say you'll marry me, live with me, love me."

"Then, yes, Lee, as-in-Willie, my not-so-imaginary friend, I will marry you and live with you and love you forever. Or until we run out of bedtime stories. Whichever comes first."

Gently, he pulled her into his arms. "Could I interest you in a bedtime story right now? I know you've had a long, upsetting day, but perhaps—"

She pressed a finger against his lips. "I need to be tucked in bed . . . with you . . . now more than ever. You were the catalyst for what happened today. I would have had to face the past and confront Emee at some point, I suppose. But when I fell in love with you, despite all my efforts not to, I had to come to terms with why I didn't want to trust you. You can't leave me alone, now. I need you with me, tonight and every night from now on."

"What about Molly?" he asked.

"She'll be fine. She needs to become accustomed to having you around, seeing you in the mornings, in the evenings . . . in my bed. *Our* bed."

A warm, welcome tenderness filled his eyes and slowly tugged at his mouth. Merry wondered if she would ever again know a moment as delicate and beautiful as this one. She'd run the gamut, from the secret pain of a past betrayal to sweet avowals of forever and she felt suddenly new. With Lee, she had found her place, her true identity. When he covered her lips in a kiss seeded with the promise of passion, she opened like a flower to his touch, accepting all he offered, forgetting everything except the healing elixir of his love.

The wineglasses stayed behind on the counter as Merry led the way down the hall to her bedroom. She paused outside Molly's room, bestowed a smile on her sleeping child, and closed the door. Turning to Lee, she wound her arms about his neck and pulled him close. "I love you." She raised her chin a bare inch and opened her mouth to invite his kiss.

He responded with a sensual investigation of her lips. He teased, toyed, and played with her tongue until a debilitating languor spread through her body. Lazily, hungrily, she reached for the buttons of his shirt and managed to separate a space wide enough for her hand to slip through. She moaned against his mouth.

"Something wrong?" He carried the delicious lassitude to the sensitive hollows of her ear.

Her head began to swim with a heady desire. "You're wearing a T-shirt under this," she said in a broken, throaty murmur. "That's not fair."

"Don't worry. It comes off." And it did . . . in two, possibly three, quick moves. She covered his bare chest in warm, wet kisses, finding the tiny nipples hidden in a tangle of hair and teasing them with her tongue. Her hand glided across the taut surface of his stomach to slide inside the waist of his jeans and caress him to a throbbing arousal. This time, he groaned and pressed her back to the wall, until all she could feel was his thighs buried against hers and the hot, thick hardness of him moving against her hand.

He found her lips and took them with a greedy kiss. She could taste his need, felt the hunger, the urgency of his passion. Her tongue dueled with his, thrusting, probing, seeking a union both physical and spiritual. She had never known such a hot, consuming desire. The sensations he evoked were familiar, but ever provocative and wildly exciting. Her hips undulated in a sensual dance, drawing him closer, tempting him with erotic promise.

"Let's get out of this hallway," he whispered as he broke the kiss to trail the tip of his tongue down her throat. He unbuttoned her blouse, nuzzled a moist path to her tingling breast and stayed there, sucking and teasing the soaked tip of her bra and the dimpled skin beneath. "Before we have to do some major explaining to Molly."

Merry nodded a weak agreement, but didn't make a move. She wasn't sure she could. Lee bent, slid his hands between her legs to part them, and then lifted her, cupping her hips and holding her as she wrapped her legs around him. A low purr escaped her lips as flesh pressed to warm and waiting flesh. The material between was a mere inconvenience. A fierce need bound them, locked them together in the knowledge that this was the true consummation of their love.

Lee pressed his open mouth to the hollow below her ear and a storm of passion swept through her. He carried her into the bedroom and stopped at the foot of the bed. Merry delighted in the scorching caress of his fingers on the curve of her hips, along the soft inner skin of her thighs. When he rubbed a seeking finger intimately against her, she gasped and leaned back. He positioned his knees on the bed and lowered her onto her back, pressing himself to her as they sank together into the give of the mattress.

She locked her arms around his neck and pulled him to her waiting lips. He came to her willingly, lost in the mystery and rapture of her love. He drank from her lips until he was consumed with the urgent need for greater sustenance. A sustenance her body offered freely and eagerly.

Clothes obeyed the sure commands of impatient fingers and without reservation or doubt, Merry explored every inch of his body, just as she encouraged him to explore hers. The caress of his hands brought her breasts to aching fullness. His breath on her skin was honey-smooth, scintillating and warm. She reached low and found the hard center of his desire and she stroked him until he quivered with need. Then, when they were both satiated with touch and throbbing with the crescendos of their own building fire, Lee moved to blanket her and end the savage torment of separation.

He entered her slowly, rocking gently into her, restraining the urgent demands of his aching body until he was anchored deep inside her. Then he moved, thrusting into the arching invitation of her hips, seeking to love her with every ounce of energy and emotion he possessed. He filled her emptiness and his own with the fierce pounding of his body until the world tilted and soared into the physical realm of ecstasy.

"I love you, Merry," he murmured as together they broke the splendid boundaries of the flesh to unite their souls in one pure and trembling moment of rapture.

For a long time afterward, she held him encircled in her arms, secure within her, knowing she had not a single doubt as to what Lee wanted from her. "I love you, Lee," she whispered against his rough cheek.

"That's my favorite bedtime story," he whispered back.

She smiled in the darkness, drew tender, sensuous circles on his chest, and began to recite, "Once upon a time, there were—"

"Can we just skip the huffing and puffing part and get right to the living happily ever after?"

"We're there, darling," she whispered. "We're already there."

HARLEQUIN *Temptation*

COMING NEXT MONTH

#305 UNDER LOCK AND KEY Cassie Miles

Molly Locke had always refused interviews regarding her
father, a world-famous writer. She wasn't about to bend the
rules for Dr. Flynn Carlson—even if he *was* the official
biographer assigned by her father's estate. Flynn was nothing
if not persistent. But Molly was convinced the handsome
biographer wanted more from her than the secrets of her past.
He wanted her....

#306 THE MAGIC TOUCH
Roseanne Williams

Brenna Deveney was a veterinarian—not a nurse! But she had
to be both when she signed on as relief vet for the injured and
bedridden Trip Hart. Tending the sexy bachelor wasn't easy; the
attraction was instantaneous—and mutual. But even more
difficult for Brenna was the realization that Trip's recovery was
in her hands . . . and her *magic*, healing touch.

#307 TEMPERATURE'S RISING
Susan Gayle

Kyla Bradford, emergency-room nurse, had had it with
snooping reporters. And Ted Spencer was no exception.
Masquerading as a patient when all he wanted was a hot story
didn't help his case. Of course, he had an infectious smile and a
very healthy body.... But when Ted's courtship started turning
into a life-threatening situation, Kyla knew she had to tend to
her heart very quickly....

#308 GLORY DAYS Marilynne Rudick

A little competition never hurt, or so Ashby and Brian O'Hara
believed. Happily married, they shared the dream of running in
the Olympics and bringing home the gold. Their "secret
weapon" was the support they got from each other—until
Ashby began to win and discovered that her success threatened
to turn their team effort into a solo affair....

THE LOVES OF A CENTURY...

Join American Romance in a nostalgic look back at the Twentieth Century—at the lives and loves of American men and women from the turn-of-the-century to the dawn of the year 2000.

Journey through the decades from the dance halls of the 1900s to the discos of the seventies ... from Glenn Miller to the Beatles ... from Valentino to Newman ... from corset to miniskirt ... from beau to Significant Other.

Relive the moments ... recapture the memories.

Look now for the CENTURY OF AMERICAN ROMANCE series in Harlequin American Romance. In one of the four American Romance titles appearing each month, for the next twelve months, we'll take you back to a decade of the Twentieth Century, where you'll relive the years and rekindle the romance of days gone by.

Don't miss a day of the CENTURY OF AMERICAN ROMANCE.

The women...the men...the passions...
the memories....

The Cowboy
JAYNE ANN KRENTZ

What better way to end a series about the search for the ideal man than with a cowboy—the enduringly popular image of the perfect hero? In June 1990, Jayne Ann Krentz brings us the third book of her exciting trilogy LADIES AND LEGENDS— THE COWBOY.

Kate, Sarah and Margaret, the three longtime friends you first met in THE PIRATE and THE ADVENTURER, are reunited in THE COWBOY—this time to see Margaret off to her mysterious encounter with Rafe Cassidy. Shrewd businessman on the surface, proud cowboy at heart, Rafe *is* the man Margaret daren't admit fantasizing about, her favorite hero come to life and waiting to make amends for the past....

THE COWBOY—available in June 1990!

T302-1

Harlequin Superromance®

A June title not to be missed....

Superromance author Judith Duncan has created her most powerfully emotional novel yet, a book about love too strong to forget and hate too painful to remember....

Risen from the ashes of her past like a phoenix, Sydney Foster knew too well the price of wisdom, especially that gained in the underbelly of the city. She'd sworn she'd never go back, but in order to embrace a future with the man she loved, she had to return to the streets...and settle an old score.

Once in a long while, you read a book that affects you so strongly, you're never the same again. Harlequin is proud to present such a book, STREETS OF FIRE by Judith Duncan (Superromance #407). Her book merits Harlequin's AWARD OF EXCELLENCE for June 1990, conferred each month to one specially selected title.

S407-1